POWER play

A MARRIAGE OF CONVENIENCE NOVELLA

ESME LENNON

SIN

CITY

Book Cover by Jules at Covers by Jules

Edited by Ria at Moon and Bloom Editing

ISBN: 9781068528316

Second edition 2025

Please note:

The Tainted Town series and The Sin City Series are intended to be a story-with-plot within a shorter book. These novellas are fast-paced and don't have as much depth as a full-length novel. This is because my novella series are written with the purpose of giving slower readers a story line to follow, plot, and spice, but with a shorter page count. Please keep this in mind while reading.

Trigger warnings

This book is intended for adult readers due to the content included.

Trigger warnings:

Mention of suicide, spanking, talk of sexual assault, blind-folding, violence/torture, stabbing, murder, alcohol, talk of drugs, drink spiking, mild bondage, explicit sex scenes, panic attacks, 8 year age gap.

For those who always doubt themselves:
You can do anything you put your mind to. Just believe in
yourself.
I believe in you.

Playlist

1. Rival – Ruelle

2. Burning in Desire – Chris Grey

3. Eyes Don't Lie – Isabel LaRosa

4. Earned It – The Weeknd

5. Again – Noah Cyrus

6. Power Over Me – Dermot Kennedy

7. Lost in the Fire – Gesaffelstein & The Weeknd

8. Under Your Skin – Seeb & R. City

9. Oh My God – Adele

10. Wicked Game – Lusaint

11. Adventure of a Lifetime – Coldplay

12. wRoNg – ZAYN (feat. Kehlani)

"In many ways, the art of love is largely the art of persistence." – Albert Ellis

Contents

POWER *play*

I hate her...
almost as much as I crave her.

1

CLAUDIA

"We have a month deadline to pay off the debt. The bank won't give us an extension or another loan. This is our lifeline, Querida."

My father's hands delicately grasp my mother's cheeks as his thumbs caress her upper cheek bones lightly. Worry and uncertainty fills his features; his chestnut brown eyes grow dull and his thick brows pull together.

"And there's nothing we can do to save our home?" My mother pleads, but the way she drops her head after the sentence leaves her mouth shows she knows there are no other options.

I swear I feel my heart break after witnessing my parents in a moment of vulnerability. My chest aches as anguish fills my body. It feels heavy, like I have weights strapped to my ankles in the middle of the sea.

I didn't know my family's financial situation was *this* bad.

One rule we've always had in my family is that we don't talk about money. My parents go out to work and always have food on the table for me and my younger brother, Thian. We never owned any designer clothing or accessories, but my wardrobe was always full and if there was anything I needed, my parents always got it for me. School supplies, education, healthcare, it's always been there for us. If it was something I wanted, then I had to earn my own money and buy it myself. As my father has always said, while we often think they come under the same category, want and need are two different things. One gets us through life, one fits into social norms.

Any money struggles my parents have had, they've hid it from us. Until now, when I stupidly decided to come downstairs for a glass of water and ended up eavesdropping on their conversation.

"There's nothing, Shannen. The owner of our apartment block is upping the price and there's nowhere else to go within our budget. I'm sorry, mi amor." My father's declaration prompts me to stop snooping and head back up to my room, ignoring my arid throat.

I swear I feel the color wash from my face. My blood feels ice cold as the realization of a struggling future smacks me in the face. I feel useless as I beg my body to remove itself from this state of shock and think of a solution.

I give myself a choice. I either sit here and drown in my own sorrows, or I switch to desperation and actually try and help my parents.

Tiptoeing my way back upstairs, my brain burns with hundreds of ideas storming through it. From gambling to becoming a stripper, ways to make money flick through my mind like a slideshow.

Swinging my wardrobe doors open so fast that a gust of wind fans me, I mentally write a list of what I could sell. Except, there's nothing. Nothing that hasn't been worn multiple times by me and nothing worth buying.

Turning around, I pick out anything else in my room worth selling.

My jewelry? I wince. *Try again, Claud.* There's not a single piece in there that's valuable. It's all sentimental pieces that cost less than ten bucks.

My laptop? I'd be fired, considering it's a company laptop and not actually mine to sell. I tried so hard to score my heritage officer trainee position, if I lost it, I'd be more of a burden to my parents than someone trying to help.

I love my job; I learn how to do the job without being sat at a college desk with paper and a pen in front of me. But I'm on a fixed contract with a fixed wage. I only get paid enough to give my parents my share of the rent and groceries. I have barely any spending money for myself left over.

Defeat engulfs me. I have nothing.

Slumping on my worthless double bed, my head finds a place in my hands. White dots blur my vision as my palms press into my eyes. My mind is a blank space, lacking in solutions.

But just when I accept my failure, a sudden memory assaults my mind. A dangerous solution that could be our family's saving grace. A stupid, and possibly useless idea that only a desperate person in need would follow up.

And that's exactly what I am.

Desperate.

I shake my head as I stare into nothingness, screaming for my sensible thoughts to come forward and talk me out of this. This is insanity. It's rational and risky, and I shouldn't even be considering it. The ache that takes over my body is fuelled by my two minds. One is telling me not to do this, but the other is screaming at me, reminding me of the fate my family will face if a solution is not sought.

I swallow, forcing the nausea that's threatening to make an appearance, down back into my stomach. Even my body is warning me of what a colossal mistake this is, but if I don't try, I'll never forgive myself.

Loud cheers echo inside one of Casamount's popular bars, The Coven, making me gulp back the anxiety creeping in my mind and focus on the main target here.

I'm not exactly dressed for the occasion in my pink and white watermelon pajama shorts and matching shirt, but my beige dust coat covers my questionable fashion choice. I show my ID, unsure of why I'm intimidated by security considering I'm twenty one, and make my way inside.

Instant loud cheers echo throughout the charcoal and turquoise themed bar as a middle-aged man sings *Highway to Hell* by AC/DC on karaoke. There isn't a free table in sight as occupiers sit, chat and drink, and the bar on the left wall is equally as busy with loud bellows of laughter and glasses being chucked forcefully into the dishwasher by staff.

My eyes scan the room as my feet stay rooted, looking for one man in particular. He's a regular here, and spends every Friday night in The Coven, so I know he's here somewhere.

A sudden low laugh comes from the bar area attracting my attention, and like the universe knew I was looking for him, I spot the one person I'm searching for. I don't give myself time to think up a plan of action before I'm pacing over towards him. His aged ivory skin shows he's sitting in the older-age category as his mousy brown and gray beard sports a short length. His green eyes are showing signs of tipsiness as they sit slightly closed and his cap hides his graying hair. He's dressed in casual clothes with a pint of beer in one hand, while using his other to gesture while he talks.

"Hi!" I exclaim, putting on a fake smile and my best flirting eyes. "Any of you fellas want to buy me a drink?" I address the three men sitting at the bar, throwing one in particular a bone.

"Sure thing, honey. A gin and tonic good for you?" His thick voice matches his elder man's look. I have to mentally stop my fist from squeezing in success as I get his attention much easier than expected.

"A beer is good for me."

"Ohh?" His brows raise in surprise.

"What?" I counter. "You've never seen a woman drink a beer before?" I tease.

"Not one as pretty as you." He winks, and I have to bite my tongue to stop myself from gagging.

He gestures to his friend to his left to move out of his seat, which he reluctantly does, and offers it to me. I sit, noting his two companions now stand behind us, but engaging in their own conversation, giving me what may be my only chance to save my family.

"What's a pretty lady like yourself doing all alone in here?" He looks around before meeting my eyes.

"To flirt with you, obviously." I emphasize the last word as the barman hands me my beer. He looks at me for payment, pointing at the card machine in front of me. "He's paying," I point to my right.

"To flirt with me, huh?" He bites his lip as he looks me up and down.

"No. Not really." I deadpan, wiping the smile off my face. Straightening my spine and lifting my chin, I keep my expression serious. "Edgar Gray, owner of the Edge Apartments block. Ruiner of lives." Venom drips from my final statement as I fight the urge to spit at him.

His flirtatious aura suddenly disappears as he frowns in confusion. "Excuse me?"

"Am I wrong?" I question.

He stutters as he struggles to defend my very correct statement.

"Look, I didn't come here for a fun night out." I lean forward, so he can hear me loud and clear. "I came to speak to you about the apartments. I overheard a conversation you had a couple weeks ago-"

He scoffs, interrupting me. "If you weren't in the conversation, it wasn't for your ears, honey."

"Hard to not be in the conversation when you speak loud enough for the whole bar to hear, *honey.*" I throw back his nickname, as I struggle to bite my tongue when my family's future sits at the forefront of my mind. "But I'm not here to argue. I heard you boasting about how much money your housing firm makes you, so obviously money is no issue for you, but it is for me and my family. We only make enough for us to get by, so you upping our payments is going to leave us homeless."

"It's the way of the world, honey. I don't make the rules." He sips his beer as he looks around, acting uninterested.

I grit my teeth at his use of honey. "Actually, you do make the rules. You're the owner, remember?"

He shrugs at my once again true statement, but doesn't offer any help. Impatience fills me as I desperately think about what I can do to solve this.

"Please, I plead. "I'll do anything."

His attention is darted back to me as his brows raise. "Anything?" He questions.

My eyes widen at the free reign I've just given him as panic claws at my insides. He must see it on my face because he laughs at me.

"Relax, I'm not some creep who's going to make you blow me to make this go away." He looks vacant as he's engrossed in his own thoughts, making each second tick by slower and slower for me. As if he's thought of the perfect plan, his eyes meet mine as a satisfied smile grows.

If anything, that smile makes me ten times more worried. God, this was a bad idea, I shouldn't be here. Is it too late to abort?

"I have a proposal for you."

"I'm listening." I say barely above a whisper, anxious to find out his plan.

"No, I have a proposal for you, like marriage." He deadpans.

I can't stop my mouth from falling open as I'm unable to form words. "Marry...you?" I say with more disgust than intended.

"God no," he waves me off. "I've been married once. Never again."

A sigh of relief leaves my lips, but it's sucked in again when I realize he still wants me to marry someone.

"My nephew. He's been a little unhinged the past few months and it's giving our family a bad name. With big businesses comes a lot of press, and we ideally want good press, not bad press."

I struggle to comprehend what he's asking of me. It's not just a 'work for me' or 'run my errands' like I was hoping. It's an actual marriage to someone I don't know, not for love.

There has to be another way. This can't be it. The word no is on the tip of my tongue as warning flags shake in my brain. I don't want this.

Tears gather in my lash line as I look at my feet, holding in a humorless laugh. I'm really considering signing away my future because there are greedy people in the world. I'm defeated and I feel pathetic, but I have no other choice.

It's to save my family.

Blinking away the tears and taking a deep breath of composure, I lift my head up. "And that's all you can offer?" I try my luck.

"That's all I can offer. I'm a billionaire, I can get pretty much anything with a snap of my fingers. This is the only thing that I've been unsuccessful in finding." He shrugs.

"And what would this mean for my family? Our payments won't increase?"

"They'll live at the Edge Apartments for free. No payment necessary."

No payment necessary rings in my ears as the resolution to my family's problem is right in front of me. No more debt and worry for my parents. A roof over their heads for the rest of their life. Yet I'm still filled with a terrible feeling in my gut.

I answer before I give my mind a chance to think logically as I nod at his agreement, "I'll need a written contract." He nods, but I need more. I need to know what I'm throwing myself into head first. "Your nephew, what's he like?"

He breathes out a laugh. "Google him. All your information is on there."

"Okay," I pause awkwardly. "What's his name?"

"Julian Gray."

Of course. The arrogant millionaire who loves no one other than himself.

Before downing my full pint, I cheers to my new future, because this one is completely different to how I envisioned it in my five year plan.

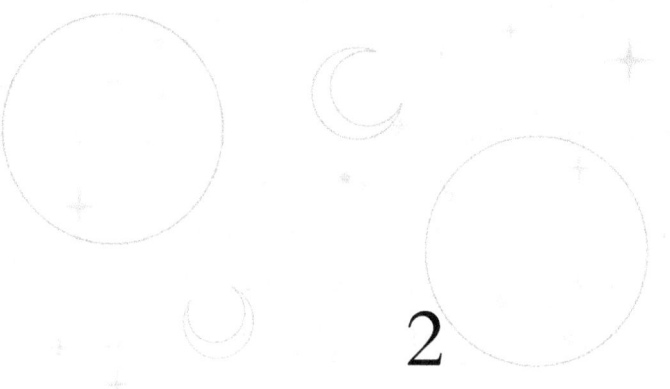

2

JULIAN

Fucking perfect. She's here, standing outside my house again. Pounding on my front door like my sleep needed interrupting.

Chucking on joggers and a t-shirt, I jog down my large, chalk white, central staircase and make my way to the double front doors.

Still pounding, I grit my teeth to suppress my annoyance. "I'm coming!" I yell, narrowing in towards the door knob. "Jesus Christ."

Pulling the door open, I'm faced with my mother, who looks me up and down with distaste. Shock fucking horror, I'm in sweats at nine in the morning. Arrest me.

"Get dressed, we're going for brunch." She flicks her long, pin straight brunette hair over her shoulder, but her slim frame causes it to fall forward again. Her brown eyes look at me sternly before glancing inside my house. Unfortunately, I inherited those exact same judgy eyes and the same brunette hair. Except I didn't get the pin straight memo, as loose waves gather on my head. "Is there someone else here with you?" Her judgey tone grates against me.

I scoff. "No." But she looks at me like I'm a liar, so I open the door wider, inviting her in so she can take a look for herself. She doesn't take me up on that invitation and stays standing on my doorstep. "Brunch isn't until eleven." I try to shut the door, but she stops it with her Louboutin heels.

"Well the Enchantment Cuisine does brunch early, so get up and get dressed, we're going out." She starts heading away from my home, shouting over her shoulder, "I'll be in the car!"

Taking a deep breath to ease the sudden oncoming headache, I shut my door and head upstairs to get myself ready.

I shower, style my hair and get dressed. Gray checkered slacks, a white shirt and loafers, and my favorite wrist watch and I feel put together for the day. I chuck on a pair of sunnies and wipe over my stubble before spritzing on some aftershave.

Making my way outside, I prepare myself for what my mother has in plan for me.

She's been plotting and constantly checking in on me the past few months, like an annoying babysitter. I've dodged every advance she's made so far, so I'm certain I can avoid this one too. I get it, she wants me to hop straight back onto the path I was on before the accident, but it's just not going to happen. I may have promised her I would change and sort myself out and make it up to her, but my life isn't what it used to be. I can't go back to how it was. Not after what I saw.

I sigh. Just another day of being the embarrassment of the family.

But one thing I will honor is the promise I made to my mother. I'm not a promise breaker, and our relationship means more to me than life itself.

My mother sits in the back of a charcoal gray Mercedes as her driver, Alfred, holds the passenger door open for me. I greet him with a nod before hopping in the back. I spend the car ride catching up on work emails, because being an owner of an investment firm takes up more of my time than I care to admit. My company is the only thing that keeps me focused and on my toes.

The Enchantment Cuisine begins coming into focus, causing me to put my phone in my breast pocket. Opening my car door before Alfred can get out of his seat, I tell him to stay seated as I jog around the back of the car and let my mother out. Grasping her hand, I help her out of the car before we make our way inside. The building is old, but its aesthetic is vintage. Palm trees and pillars compliment the cream brick and black paint exterior, with a large sign above the doorway saying 'Enchantment Cuisine'. A few black metal tables and chairs sit outside the large windows, all occupied by early brunch attendees.

As we make our way inside the large double doors, an employee greets us, waving us on through. We're regulars here, and booking is never necessary when we arrive. The open plan interior creates a lively vibe, with the cream brick theme following. Large overhanging lights create a glow, and is a beautiful contrast with the black table and chairs. An oval central bar sits in the middle of the room, with employees whisking away drinks to different tables.

My jaw instantly clenches at the sight of my uncle sitting at our regular table at the back center of the room. My mother's plotting is irritating enough, but my uncle teaming up with her can only mean bad things. I didn't prepare for this.

"Edgar," I hiss. "What a surprise."

"Take a seat, Julian. We have business." He gestures to the seat opposite him, as my mother takes the seat in between us on the circular table.

Once I sit, a young redhead comes to take our order. I settle for avocado bagels and black coffee before doing my best to look uninterested. I observe the restaurant, listen in on people's conversations, I even focus on the wall detail. I'm already fucking bored.

"So," my uncle begins. "Business."

My mother side eyes him as her eyes widen. "Let him have his brunch first." I inhale a deep breath with my eyes closed. Their sibling quarrels get worse as they get older.

"I don't want him to throw boiling hot coffee at me."

A frown assaults my face. "Why would I do that?" I question, inching my face forward to hear his answer.

They both look between each other, making my patience grow thin. My jaw clenches and my fists ball together. I'm three seconds away from leaving. "What the fuck is this?" I growl.

"Julian, you can't carry on like this. It's giving us a bad name and we won't stand for it any longer." My uncle's voice is now stern as his face turns stoic. "Partying, getting into fights, you name it."

I huff out a laugh. "I go out drinking with my friends to have fun like a normal twenty nine year old." I shake my head. "And the *few* fights were nothing. Just men putting their hands on women who said no. They deserved it."

"Twenty nine year olds are usually settled down by now. You know, marriage, kids."

"Neither of you two are married." I flick my finger in between my mother and uncle. "And that was the norm twenty years ago, not now."

"Enough." My uncle's fist bangs the table, making the cutlery clatter. Eyes around us find our table, causing my uncle and mother both to readjust their cutlery, making it look intentional. "This is it, Julian."

My brows furrow together as I try to figure out what he means. My mother's hand is placed on top of mine, making my eyes dart to hers.

"You made me a promise, baby. Please, just do it." She pauses as sadness coats her eyes. "For me."

"Do what?" I exclaim, confused.

"You're getting married-"

"What?" I recoil, interrupting my uncle's bizarre and untrue statement. "No, I'm not." I shake my head repeatedly.

"Yes, you are. She's great. Beautiful and focused."

My head reels in shock as I fail to accept the fact that not only am I supposedly getting married, but she's already been chosen for me. Someone I don't know, have never met, and have no desire to be with. Betrayal fills me as my blood runs hot.

"You can't just choose a wife for me! It's not how it works!" Anger radiates off my body, causing my mother to retract her hand.

My uncle nods, "It's the only way, Julian." His eyes glance at my mother and I know he's referring to the foolish fucking promise.

"No," I turned my attention to my mother. "Choose another way for me to make it up to you."

"Edgar's right." She smiles guiltily. "It's the only way."

My mind is swarming with assaulting thoughts, unable to get them in order. The minor headache has now turned into a full blown migraine, while my vision can only see red. Betrayal always hurts more when it's from someone you love and trust. I'm grateful for the fury bubbling inside of me, because it distracts me from how the betrayal hurts my heart.

I don't bother waiting for my food to arrive as I rise to my feet. I turn on the ball of my foot to walk away, but it hits me that I didn't ask the most important question.

I turn to face them both, ignoring the remorse lining their faces. "Who is it?"

My uncle clears his throat, "Claudia Ibáñez."

☼ • ☼ • ☼ • ☼

It took me a quick Facebook search to find her location. Her friend, Amalie, posted a photo of them at The Coven, giving me exactly what I needed.

I dress in a casual t-shirt and jeans, sporting a black cap to keep my identity somewhat hidden. It's not my usual spot, so I'm hoping I won't know anyone. I just want to watch my soon to be wife.

The thought makes me grit my teeth. I'm fucking furious at my mother and uncle, but I'm more resentful towards myself for even trying to convince myself to go through with this. My brain is telling me a million reasons why this is a fucking stupid idea, but my heart is screaming louder, reminding myself of the laughable promise I made. Laughable because I couldn't pull myself together enough for my mother, so now my fate has been chosen for me. I don't want to accept it, but what other choice do I have?

I order a beer and sit at the corner of the bar, having perfect eye line to the dance floor. I observe my surroundings, looking for one person in particular, but I'm yet to succeed. The bar is busy, which is expected for a Saturday night, but it also helps my cause to stay hidden.

Flashing lights assault my vision as pop music plays through large speakers, causing people to sing and cheer. The loudness makes my head hurt, and I'm so fucking tempted to abort mission when a flash of green catches my eye. The green dress Amalie was wearing in the Facebook photo. My eyes zero in, looking for the long, black, straight hair I recognize from Claudia's online profile.

I find nothing as irritance claws at my insides. I pick up my beer and turn my head to take a large sip, but just as the glass meets my lips, I pull it away and turn back to Amalie. Because with Amalie, is Claudia.

A gorgeous smile with luscious lips, beautiful ocean blue eyes, taller than Amalie, but still shorter than me. Her slim figure looks exquisite in her tight black dress, giving me a perfect image of her ample cleavage and plump ass.

Beautiful isn't enough to describe her.

She is divine. Ravishing. Elegant. A sight for sore eyes.

Fuck. I hate her already.

I take my time watching her as I prepare myself for my new future. Does she know? Of course she knows. I fucking hope she does, anyway.

Claudia sways her hips to the music, her movements sexy and seductive.

It could've been worse, I guess. At least if everything else fails in our marriage, I have a wife who's nice to look at. Shrugging, I accept that thought as a positive. But just like a flick of a switch, my positive thinking turns to negative when I see a scrawny guy grasp Claudia's hips, pulling her close.

I rise to my feet, disgust coursing through me as another guy tries to harass women when they have no goddamn right, but she turns to face him and wraps her arms around his neck, dancing with him. She smiles at him as he whispers something in her ear, and his hands snake around her hips.

This day is just full of fucking annoyance. Even my soon to be wife fucking betrays me. With some guy who doesn't even look old enough to be in here.

Downing my cheap, shitty beer, I storm out the door, not giving Claudia one more glance.

Welcome to my own personal hell.

3

CLAUDIA

Sometimes I question my own logical thinking, wondering how the hell I end up in situations that I should've avoided like the flu. I know I should stand back and think about a situation before I dive in head first, but I'm a doer, not a thinker. It's easier to ask for forgiveness than permission, which is why I do it now and worry about it later.

I have no clue how I'm going to explain to my parents that I'm getting married. I've never even had a serious boyfriend before, let alone taking myself off the market for a marriage. They're going to kill me.

I inhale a deep sigh. I know I need to tell them the truth, but I'm just not ready yet. I haven't even come to terms with what's happening in my life, and I know they'll have questions, so it's better for me to hold off until I have all the answers. Or an answer that'll satisfy them.

After having the hottest shower I could tolerate and adding some light makeup to my face, I clip half my hair up in a bow at the back of my head, and chuck on some clothes. I settle for a dusk brown pinafore dress, a black long sleeved sweater and thick black tights, adding my favorite leather black Chelsea boots. Slinging my slate gray duster coat over my shoulders, I grab my handbag and head out the front door.

I avoid my parents easily; living in this house for twenty one years means I've perfected sneaking around. I could tell them I'm going out with friends, but I don't like lying to them. This way, I just don't have to tell the truth.

The truth is, I'm heading to Edgar Gray's home to sign the contract. You know, the one that signs my single life away. My chance of finding real love is now gone with the wind, because I'm giving myself to Julian Gray.

I groan. Even his name makes my mood sour.

To make matters worse, I'm also meeting Julian for the first time and that thought alone makes me irritable. But I do a few breathing techniques to calm myself down and to keep my composure, because I can't mess this up. This is for my family, the only outcome I can afford right now is this contract working out.

I call a cab to come and collect me, and I spend the fifteen minute drive trying not to overthink. Distracting my mind is as hard as algebra, and I scored straight A's in math. I'm speaking to my own brain like I'm worried someone can read my mind and I have to come up with anything to make myself seem normal. Do I need to do laundry when I'm home? What days are hair wash days this week? Should I get a dog? How would you give a giraffe CPR?

The distraction works a treat until I arrive at my location. I hop out the cab and the air shifts around me. This part of Casamount feels like a different country. The houses here are modern mansions, all four floors minimum, with spacious gardens and lengthy drives. There are gardeners driving around on golf buggies, attending to different gardens, keeping them in perfect shape. The cars look like they cost more than an average housing block, and each home has a post outside of it stating who lives there. It looks like a movie scene, one where the neighborhood all purge or turn into psychopaths. Not the vibe I'm wanting.

Edgar Gray's home is a five story, sand coloured mansion with a circular driveway and a water fountain in the middle.

There are three garages to the left of the home and in the center is a large staircase that leads to the front double doors.

I gulp at how beautifully intimidating it looks, but then I'm fueled with anger at the realization that he's living comfortably in this gorgeous house, yet my family is barely able to make enough money for rent. For the damn housing estate Edgar owns. I don't care if it's the way the world works, it's fucking cruel. And now I have to marry a grumpy asshole because his uncle is greedy.

Live and let live, I guess.

Taking the brick stairs to the front door, I ball my fist up and rasp lightly, before deciding on having little respect and knocking loudly. I can hear distant footsteps, but they sound so far away. Distant shouting then follows, and it takes me at least eight seconds to realize it's Edgar shouting 'I'm coming'. His silhouette is visible through the blurred glass on the front doors as he paces down the staircase, before opening the door for me.

"Ah! Miss Claudia, come on in." He smiles with his blinding teeth as he steps aside, letting me pass.

Well, at least I'm still a Miss...for now.

I offer him a nod in greeting, my words suddenly unable to form. I'm very much aware of how bad this idea is, but I don't let myself dwell on it. It's not an option to think myself out of this.

Edgar guides me towards a large room at the back of the home, with a large rectangular marble table placed in the middle, more than enough chairs surrounding it, with breathtaking artwork covering the walls. It ranges from O'Keefe to El Greco, and I don't doubt these are original paintings. Renaissance art covers the ceiling, with a gold and pale pink theme running throughout, which also matches the gold portable bar trolleys dotted around the room.

"Drink?" Edgar pulls me from my art induced daydream as he points towards a drinks trolley.

"Please," I respond. I'm not a big drinker, but I'm going to need some liquid courage to get through this.

As liquid sloshes in the background, I try to make the awkward silence a little less awkward.

"Are these originals?" I point to the paintings on the wall.

"Mmhm." Edgar nods as he passes me a crystal glass with amber liquid inside. "As a collector, I pride myself on the paintings I own. They took a lot of trouble to own."

"I don't doubt that. They probably cost more than The Great Pyramid of Giza."

His light chuckle loosens the lingering tension in the room. "I'm sure you'd know, as a history buff."

My eyes squint at his response before a smile curves at my lips. "Someone's been doing their homework."

"I like to know who I'm introducing into my family."

"Well," I take a few steps towards him. "I'm no genius, but homework should be completed before you walk in, I don't know," I wave my hand in a circle, "a marriage."

We both laugh softly, but the calming vibe that surrounds the room is quickly shattered by the sound of the front door slamming and distant angry words. I can't make out much due to the sheer size of Edgar's home, but I can understand 'never wanted this' and 'better be worth it'. I gulp nervously as sudden anxiety consumes me as I realize who entered the house.

Julian.

Ice washes over me as my body tenses up. The warm conversation that took place mere seconds ago is long gone. It's replaced with distance and rigidness as Julian enters the room. I can't stop my head from turning in his direction and drinking in his appearance.

Tall, handsome, and stoic.

The room feels like it drops below zero degrees when he walks in as he sucks out all feeling of comfort and fervor.

My natural response is to run and avoid a person with such nature. I'm damn near doing it until my phone flashes up in my hand. A call from my mother as a family photo flashes on my screen. An immediate reminder this is for them. I sigh and send the call to voicemail. God, I hope she never finds out about this.

Stealing my spine, I lift my chin and turn towards him. I'm thankful the large dining room table separates us as I pretend I'm confident and calm.

Edgar breaks the deafening silence, instructing us to take a seat. I pause for a second, letting Edgar take his seat first, so I can sit next to him and not Julian. He sits himself at the head of the table, Julian on his left, so I take a seat at Edgar's right. Opposite Julian.

He's even more handsome up close.

Focus, Claud. Be thankful you have a soon-to-be husband that's pleasant to look at.

"Julian, Claudia." Edgar's hand goes from Julian to me. "Claudia, Julian."

Silence.

Edgar clears his throat, interrupting the once again painful stillness. "Now we have the formalities out of the way, let's talk business. This marriage may be arranged, but that isn't going to stop you both from acting like you're in love. The Gray name holds a high social standard and neither of you are going to tarnish it. I expect you both to respect the Gray name and this marriage. That means no putting on a show for paparazzi, no wild nights out with drinking and drugs, and no disrespecting each other."

Sliding two small stacks of papers to us both, Edgar proceeds. "Here are your contracts; read and sign." He hands us both a fancy golden pen with 'Gray Investments' written in bold letters.

Time goes by painfully slowly as I read every word of the contract. I can't afford anything less than my standards in this commitment.

Taking in everything I read, Edgar surprisingly wrote a good contract. No secrets, no sly rules, just a well written arranged marriage contract.

Yikes. Sounds worse than I'd wanted.

Julian taps his pen impatiently on the marble table as he lets out impatient breaths. I check the clock on the far wall and notice it's taken me an hour to read through the whole thing.

His inattention to detail is slightly concerning, considering he signed it less than ten minutes after Edgar gave it to us. I'm not sure if I should be worried he signed so fast, or impressed that he can apparently read that fast.

Taking a breath of composure, I scribble my signature along the dotted line and pass the papers back over to Edgar.

Twenty pieces of paper. That's all it takes to write my new future.

Picking the papers up and tapping them on the table so they're all aligned with each other, Edgar places them down in front of him as he swigs his whiskey. "Okay," he nods, "congratulations on your engagement. I wish you a lifetime of happiness."

Sarcasm laces his voice, causing me to down the untouched amber liquid in my glass.

"The wedding will be in three months, until then, you will get to know each other."

Edgar's voice is beginning to grate on me as he lays out more rules for my dream come true. "Julian, Claudia will need a ring, I'm trusting you to take care of it."

Julian's nod is barely noticeable as his face remains irritated.

"You can sort living arrangements between you both," Edgar's chair squeaks as he rises to his feet. "I'm not staying in this room a minute longer, you're both sucking the energy out of it."

I bite my tongue to stop myself from making a sarcastic remark. I want to tell Edgar I'm sorry I'm not my happiest while being signed over to his annoying nephew because of his greediness.

But I don't.

"Oh," Edgar stops by the large archway just before he leaves the room. "And it goes without saying, absolutely no cheating on each other. The paps love that shit. Any relationships, situationships, fuck-and-chucks all end now. This is to be a faithful marriage."

Edgar's departure is welcomed, but the scoff that leaves Julian's mouth isn't.

Tilting my head to the side, my frown is uncontrollable. "Something funny?" I question.

"Edgar's no cheating rule has *got* to be a bitch for you." He meets my stare as he rests his forearms on the table, fingers interlocked. "No more dry humping sweaty boys at The Coven."

My frown drops as anger courses through me at the realization he saw me last weekend.

"Are you stalking me?" I spit, my irritation at the forefront of my mind. I match his posture with my arms on the table, but they're no where near a match for his muscular forearms and large biceps straining against his white shirt.

"Stalking you?" His bitter tone is insulting. "Honey, I'd rather scrape my dick on a cheese grater."

I wince. "Charming. I'm marrying an asshole."

"I'm as thrilled as you are about this marriage."

I don't know why, but his words sting. Rising to my feet, I grab my bag and set my eyes on the front door.

"We aren't finished." Julian's abrupt tone makes me halt my steps. I want to be gone of his negative attitude, but I see him writing on a piece of paper, piquing my interest.

He slides the paper over to me and rises to his feet. "That's my address. Meet me there in ten so we can discuss arrangements."

I grimace. "We're going separately?"

"Yes. Find your own ride."

And in a flash, he's already at the door and leaving.

A breath of annoyance leaves my body as I come to terms with what just happened.

I'm marrying a self-centered asshole.

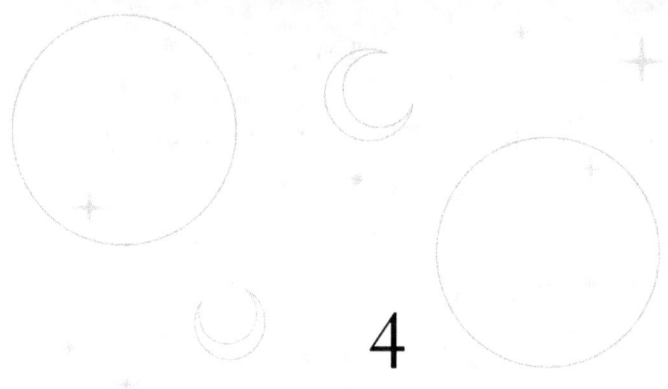

4

JULIAN

My patience is running thin today. My new fiancée is stubborn, annoying and bothersome. Having her within my vicinity is going to be the bane of my life. Given, she's appealing to look at, but that doesn't mask her rude tone and bluntness.

Once Edgar's large front door slams behind me, I allow myself my first deep breath of the day. A thick headache pounds at my skull, reminding me I've not once hydrated myself today. Ring shopping, an early morning gym session and a business meeting has given me little time to worry about my needs, and while now would be a perfect time to go home and sink myself into my work, I have an unwanted guest arriving in exactly nine minutes and twenty-seven seconds.

My charcoal gray Mercedes S Class is brought around by Edgar's valet driver and I make quick work of hopping in and driving home. I live a short five minute drive from Edgar's home, so I make it back with four minutes to spare. I head into my open plan kitchen and pour myself a glass of water before heading into my home office. The steel and gold theme throughout adds light to the room, creating a positive and focused workspace for me. A large desk is placed opposite my office window, with shelving covering three walls. The final wall has a centered window and two art pieces hanging either side. Original Picasso paintings.

Logging on, I note my fiancée has a minute left until her expected arrival. The chair opposite my desk awaits her as I sit back and relax, flicking through work emails on my laptop.

Checking the clock again, Claudia's ten minute deadline was up fifteen minutes ago. Irritation causes my molars to grind together as I rise to my feet at her lateness. If there's one thing I hate, it's impracticality. It's not hard to be on time, and in my line of work, it's a must.

She's going to be the death of me.

The distant voices pull my attention as I head to the front door to see what the problem is. As I investigate further, I see Claudia at the front gate, jabbing random numbers into my gate lock as my groundskeeper kindly advises her to stop before it heads into system failure.

He's not wrong, so I pace down my long driveway to come face to face with Claudia through metal gate poles.

"What are you doing?" I hiss, not helping her further.

She throws her arms up in frustration. "Do you expect us to have this conversation through a gate?" She jabs, her annoyance clear on her frowning expression.

"Why didn't you just press the buzzer?" I point to the clear 'entry request' buzzer above the gate keypad.

Her ocean blue eyes dart to the buzzer before meeting mine, shrugging her shoulders. "I didn't realize I'd need permission to enter my soon-to-be husband's home."

Sighing at her petty response, I can feel the irritance growing in my shoulders. "If it means you'll stop trying to cause a system failure and shouting at my groundsman, then you can have the code." I unlock the gate by pressing the buttons on the keypad on my side of the gate, silently cursing myself for not bringing the key fob with me. As the gate opens, I begin striding back up my driveway, not waiting for her to enter. "The code was going to be given to you once we had our meeting, which was scheduled twenty minutes ago. You're late."

"I had to find my own ride, remember." She catches up to me as we enter my home. "Some asshole expected me to call an uber, wait for it to arrive and make my way to his home in less than ten minutes."

"He sounds great," I counter. Her huff of disapproval has me feeling accomplished.

Shutting the door behind her, I lead her into my office and gesture to the chair opposite my desk for her to sit. She places her bag down beside her and takes a seat, sitting with her back straight and legs crossed, like a perfect lady. Shame her mouth has to ruin it.

Once I sit, I pull a business card from my top drawer and write down the gate code, before sliding it over to her. "Code is 2703. Don't lose it, I won't be telling you the code again."

She looks over the code before nodding and placing it into her bag. Before she looks up, I place a ring box in front of her. "This is your engagement ring. Wear it at all times, I don't need the paparazzi making up any stories."

She opens the box, almost immediately gulping as white washes over her olive skin. She stutters as she pulls the golden band from the cushioned box. The swiss blue topaz stone gleams in the sunlight shining through the window, almost blinding me.

"How much?" She breathes.

"$300,000, so don't lose it. I'm not buying another." I respond abruptly as she gawks at it. Jesus, has this girl never seen money before?

I doubt myself as I think I saw a tear well in her eye, but she blinks it away almost instantly. Sliding the ring onto her finger, it fits perfectly and compliments her skin tone.

"How do you know my size?" She questions as she steals her spine, suddenly overcoming whatever emotional moment she just had.

"It's a gift. I'm a good guesser."

"Not bad." Claudia nods, her face suddenly back to its usual straightness. "Thank you."

Nodding at what I assume was a compliment, I pull up the notes I wrote on my laptop before she arrived, reminding me what this meeting is for. "You're a heritage officer, correct?" She nods. "I'm unsure on how a job like that occupies your time, but my work is twenty-four-seven. I spend a lot of time at the Gray Investments building in the city, and the rest of my time is spent here in my office, so we won't cross paths often."

"You could ask." She interrupts me, giving me a snarky look.

"Ask what?" I frown.

"What my job entails."

"But then I'd have to pretend to care." I counter.

She scoffs, shaking her head. "Asshole."

"Do you have a kink I should be aware of?" I question, noticing her choice of insults always seem to be asshole.

Claudia recoils, her frown now more prominent. "What? No!" She defends.

"It was a joke." I nod, focusing my attention back on my laptop.

"Didn't realize you were capable of those."

Her wit is funny, but I hold in my laugh. "Living arrangements," I proceed. "You'll move in here tomorrow. Choose a bedroom, there's fifteen to choose from."

"Minus yours?" She questions, her nose curling up like she's disgusted mine is included in the bedroom choice.

"Minus mine." I confirm.

She clears her throat, resting her forearms on my desk as she leans forward. "And how am I supposed to explain to my parents I'm moving out and into my soon to be husband's home?"

I shrug. "Not my problem." I make a mental note to do some research on my fiancée's background.

"Fine." She sits back in her seat. "But I get to go home on weekends. I need some sort of break from you and your stupidly big mansion."

I'm about to protest, but a weekend break from her actually sounds like a good idea. "Fine. But only weekends."

She nods in agreement.

"You'll have a driver." I proceed, flicking through my notes.

She shakes her head, her eyes rolling. "A driver? Seriously? Mr 'I have money growing out my ass'."

"Again with the ass-" I'm interrupted by her death glare. "You'll have a driver take you wherever you need. His name is Adrian, here's his number for you to call whenever you need." I write the digits on another business card and slide it over to her.

"I've been getting around just fine without a chauffeur." She protests.

"Not in this neighborhood you haven't. You're going to be a Gray, you need to start living, and acting, like one."

Her scoff of disapproval is immediate, but she doesn't argue further. So, she can bite her tongue sometimes. Good to know.

"Movers will be at your place at twelve PM sharp-"

"Let me deal with the move." Claudia interrupts as she breathes a heavy sigh. Her shoulders drop in what looks like defeat, but I don't read too much into it. "It'll be too stressful for my parents to try and understand what's going on here. I'll get my bags ready and take them out one by one to the movers," she points her index finger at me, "who cannot be in view of my home. This needs to be done as quietly and discreetly as possible."

Thoughts invade my mind as I try to piece together why she can't just tell her parents what's going on, but then I realize this isn't exactly a typical marriage. My mother forced me into this because of a promise, I don't have a clue why Claudia is partaking in this marriage. That I'll need to find out.

Nodding, I agree to her terms. "They'll park out of view from your home, I'll inform them on how this will work."

"Thank you." She offers a slight smile, and the softness offers me a peek of a different side of her. Calm, sweet and adorable.

I evict that thought from my mind immediately.

Noting I've come to the end of my list, I close my laptop and clasp my hands together. "That's all."

Claudia's brows dart upwards quickly as a form of agreement as she rises to her feet. I mirror her, standing up and walking around the desk. Just as I'm about to walk past her, she bends in front of me to pick up her bag, before slinging it on her shoulder. I clear my throat, her back mere centimeters from my front. We're so close I can feel the heat radiating from her body as I tower over her.

Turning instantly to see what the issue is, Claudia's cheeks bloom pink as her eyes meet mine, before looking at the very little space between us. Stepping away like I'm a walking STD, she whispers a barely audible apology before walking towards the door. I bite my cheek to hide the smirk that's desperate to appear.

I'm sure she's suddenly intent on running a race as she tries her hardest to speed away from me, but my strides match her rushed steps. Her hand reaches for the door knob, but mine gets there first, and I open the door for her. She's already halfway down the driveway when she shouts "see you tomorrow," before keying in the code and leaving my home in her rear vision.

I shut the door once Claudia is out of vision. Dialing my PA, Ferne, I instruct her to arrange movers for tomorrow, ready for what could possibly be the biggest mistake of my life.

5

CLAUDIA

He may be a dick, but he has a nice home, which infuriates me more. My parents are living in a basic apartment complex when Julian and his family see money as just a piece of paper. It's my family's lifeline, and it hurts to see people not give a care in the world.

That's why you're marrying him, Claud.

I almost choked on air when I entered Julian's home. The foyer itself is bigger than our whole apartment alone. The white exterior and the pillars were enough for me to know his home was going to be like a palace, but to house sixteen bedrooms, an office, and god knows what other rooms, had my mouth falling agape.

Rooms exit off the foyer, too many to count, and the large central staircase looked like a royal dream. He has an actual corridor leading to his office. I was tempted to ask for a house tour, but it meant spending more time with him, and that sounded more like a nightmare. His driveway was long enough to give me a stitch, and his lawn surrounds the front of his home. Kudos to his groundman, he keeps it in excellent condition.

The two original Picasso paintings in his office caught my attention immediately, but I didn't want to boost his ego by gushing over them. I'll find a way to admire them up close sooner or later, without Julian's hateful presence.

My mind had whiplash as soon as Julian mentioned living here. I don't want to *live* here, and I don't know why I didn't even consider that would be the plan, considering our marriage. My past with men has been painful, and the thought of sharing a home with one makes my blood run cold. But I push it to the back of my mind and remind myself what this is for.

Plus, I get my own space. A safe space for me to keep myself protected and secure. A choice of fifteen bedrooms, I shake my head at the reminder of my internal excitement, I plan to choose the biggest and the furthest away from Julian's room.

The more distance between us, the safer I'll feel at night time and the more I can avoid his existence.

I pack the basics that I'll need to take to Julian's; underwear, work clothes, toothbrush. I realize how little I travel when I run out of bag space after packing a quarter of the things I need. Trash-bags it is.

Stuffing everything I think I'll need inside, I'm satisfied with what I've got. I take one last glance around the room, when light-blue catches my eye. I gulp as my vibrator looks back at me, almost challenging me to leave it behind. Julian frustrates me, and the best way to release frustration is to orgasm, right? I quickly dash to my bedside drawer and grab it, stuffing it into a bag.

Taking one last glance at my bedroom, I shut the door behind me, reminding myself I'll be back in five days.

My parents are sitting in the living room together, watching an old black and white movie. My father's arm is wrapped around my mother's shoulder as she feeds him popcorn, giggling in unison.

Warmth engulfs me as I watch them in their bubble, but it's quickly replaced by sadness. I don't want to leave and miss out on loving moments like these. Emptiness also smacks me in the face when I realize I'll never have a love like them. I'll just have a loveless marriage, filled with misery and venom.

Blinking the tears from my eyes, I take a deep breath and carry my things outside to the movers. They wait out of view of my home like requested. At least I know Julian can follow orders.

I plead with them to wait ten more minutes while I say goodbye to my parents, and head back to my home. Anxiety fills my stomach as I mentally prepare myself to lie to them in order to protect them from the truth.

Entering my home in silence like I perfected when I was fourteen, I make my way to the living room and sit down opposite my parents.

"Hola, Nena." My father passes me the bowl of popcorn, but I shake my head in refusal. If I eat now, I'll probably throw up.

"There are some buildings over in Charlestown that need to be inspected, and work have insisted I stay in hotels during the week instead of commuting every day." I start off explaining, trying my hardest to hold eye contact.

"So you won't be here this week?" My mother questions, sitting forward as she engulfs herself in our conversation.

"Well it's a large workload and they aren't sure how long it'll take, so for some time I'll only be home at weekends."

"Oh baby," my mother's sadness makes me want to swallow my lies and tell the truth. "Is there no other way? We'll miss you."

I shake my head as my brows pull together in anguish. "Trust me, I'd have already chosen it if there was, but it's my job and I have to do it. I'm sorry Mamá."

"Hey, it's okay, Claud. We'll miss you around here but we understand. We'll look forward to the weekends each week." My father reaches for my hand across the table and squeezes it, giving me comfort. "I'll make empanadas for you when you're home."

"Gracias, Papá." Nothing beats his empanadas. My father has always made sure me and Thian don't miss out on the Argentinian traditions he had growing up.

I rise to my feet, my parents mirroring me and pulling me into a group hug. My father places a delicate kiss on my forehead before releasing me. Just as I'm about to let go of my mother, Thian runs into the room and joins us.

This just keeps getting harder.

I release them both and bend to Thian's level, grasping his hands. "I've got to go away for work for a few days, but I'll be back on Friday, okay?"

"Promise?" Thian holds up his pinky.

I interlock my pinky with his, sealing the deal. "Promise."

Placing my suede boots on my feet, I head for the door.

"Where's your things, honey?" My mother questions, and I internally curse myself for not thinking this through.

"Oh, they're outside already! A friend from work is picking me up."

Before I make this situation even worse, I leave, waving to them as I round the corner out of their vision.

Arriving at Julian's home is the start of my own depressing movie. This is the beginning of my terrible new life, I want to stand in front of the movers truck to put me out of my misery. Except they're stationary so the damage will be non-existent.

After pleading with movers to let me carry a bag, and them refusing profusely, I make my way inside Julian's home. His

Mercedes isn't parked outside, so I'm guessing (hoping) that means he's not here.

That leads me to my next problem; how am I supposed to know which room is his? I could search all sixteen bedrooms, but knowing my luck, it'll be the last room I check.

What could only be described as a bird's nest of hair catches my attention. An older woman carrying a duster waltzes into the room, humming a song.

"Excuse me," I smile, holding my hand out to stop her. "Can you tell me which one is Julian's bedroom? I don't want to intrude."

"Hello, my pretty!" Her sudden happiness catches me by surprise. I didn't think Julian would want anyone with a smile around him. "I'm Magda, Julian's housekeeper." She places her hands on both my cheeks, tucking the duster under her arm. "My my, you're a pretty thing, aren't you? Julian has really outdone himself!"

"Oh," I wave her off, unsure of how much she knows about our situation. "I'm flattered."

"Julian's bedroom is the furthest room on the left wing." She squeezes my cheeks one last time before grabbing her duster and moving to another room, not even giving me a chance to thank her.

Turning to the movers behind me who are still carrying in my belongings, I say, "Furthest room on the right wing, please," before heading up the stairs.

Julian's taste isn't what I thought it would be. I was expecting red and black, with pictures of satan hanging on the walls, but instead, it's gold and white with splashes of pink lemonade throughout. I can see Edgar's taste for Renaissance runs in the family, as it seems to be Julian's taste too, as it covers the ceiling of the foyer and upstairs hallway. The white marble flooring runs up the stairs and along the lengthy hallway, with a white and golden speckled carpet along the center. Julian doesn't need a red carpet when he has this gorgeous one under his feet. Original paintings cover the walls as doors assault my vision. There's too many to count, and I'd be here all week if I wanted to look inside them all.

My eyes dart to the left wing as I faintly smell Julian's scent in the air. Tobacco and cinnamon invades my nostrils as I inhale deeply. That's a big enough warning for me to turn right.

Once I make it towards the end of the corridor, I catch myself breathing deeper. I feel like I've walked up a hill for twenty-minutes; this house is unnecessarily *big*. I'm not unfit; my job requires a lot of walking around as I survey old buildings, but living in this house requires constant cardio, which I'm sure Julian does, considering the devil never sleeps.

The large white door stares down at me as I grip the golden, circular door knob. I twist and push the door open cautiously, expecting to be faced with a thousand nightmares. Instead, it's classic decor and exquisite taste. A four post bed with sheer white curtains, pastel pink and gold Renaissance canvas the ceiling, all white furniture with golden decorative items attached, and a beautiful marble dressing table with a golden frame circular mirror. There's a large walk-in wardrobe to my right and an en-suite bathroom to my left. The same decor theme runs throughout the bathroom, screaming Renaissance and elegance, and I find myself having to catch my breath at how stunning it is.

Julian definitely didn't have a decorative say in this, right? There's no way in hell we have *anything*, like decorative taste, in common.

I glance at the bedroom door and notice the lock, nodding my reassurance. Safety is always important, and I'm glad the lock is there if I ever feel the need to use it. Hushed voices snap me out of my creative daze as the movers begin delivering my belongings. I insist they leave them outside my room so it doesn't turn into a muddled mess, and before I know it, a quarter of the corridor is bags of my things. I didn't think I brought a lot of things with me, but the movers unload more than a dozen bags. Oops.

I hurl a mix between *thank-yous* and *sorrys* at them as I notice their blushed cheeks and the sweat beading on their foreheads. My things would still be downstairs if I had to bring them up here. I would've been exhausted after bag one.

Who are you trying to fool, Claud? You were exhausted from just walking to your room.

Digging my phone out from my bag, I flick through my music playlist. Panic at the Disco's *Miss Jackson* starts playing, leaving me, good music and my belongings to get organized.

I'm fully engrossed in unpacking my things when a low voice catches me off guard, causing me to yelp. My hands find my chest as I feel my heart thud from the sudden surprise.

Julian stands at the doorway, one shoulder leaning against the frame as he crosses his arms. His shirt sleeves are rolled up, showing his toned lower arms and veiny hands. He obviously finds my panic funny as he lets out a light chuckle.

"Not funny," I demand, crossing my arms in annoyance. "I didn't know you were capable of smiling." My eyebrows raise in fake shock.

"It won't happen again." He deadpans, the smile disappearing from his face. I don't doubt he's lying either.

"You know, you could've brought me a bag before you stepped over all my things." It's only just occurred to me that he must have played a game of twister as he stepped over all my belongings.

"Could've," he shrugs, "but didn't." His eyes glance at all my belongings before focusing back on me, suddenly making me feel small. "I'd hoped I'd got lucky and you decided not to go through with this, but obviously not."

"It's a bad day for us both." I focus back on organizing my things.

A sigh escapes Julian's lips before he attempts to turn around without stepping on anything, "And I'm not going to make my day any worse by staying here-"

He's suddenly cut short by a low buzz coming from one of my bags.

Heat blooms on my face as panic washes over me, freezing me to the spot. I know exactly what that noise is. I tell my legs to move, to dart over to my bags and find the source of my embarrassment, but they won't comply. Internally, I beg the ground to swallow me whole and spit me out far away from here.

Julian's gaze goes from a bag next to his feet, over to me, then back to the bag. Before I could rush over to stop him, he reaches down and pulls his hand out with my blue vibrator nestled inside his grip.

Fuck. My. Life.

"This is my competition?" Julian eyes my bedtime friend curiously before darting his gaze over to me. His eyes change from emotionless and cold to something I'm unsure of. Temptation?

Nope. Not going there.

My face suddenly feels like a flame is in front of me as shame makes my whole body sweat. Out of all the bad things that could've happened, I definitely wasn't expecting this.

Striding over towards me, Julian holds out my vibrator towards me. My hands couldn't clasp around it soon enough, but he doesn't release it straight away. He just holds onto it with a tight grip and stares at me fiercely, like he can see all my sins.

"Good to know." He speaks an octave above a whisper, a smirk threatening to pull at his peachy lips. But before I can read into what the fuck just happened, Julian lets go and is completely out of sight. No longer in my room, not in the hallway, and definitely not holding my vibrator.

6

CLAUDIA

The best way to get over embarrassment? Drink it away with cheap beer.

I wince at the recurring memory of what happened a week ago, begging my mind to forget it like it's a distant memory, but it stays glued to the front of my mind.

I'm tempted to contact the company and claim my vibrator is faulty. Why else would it go off on its own accord? Karma chose me as its victim that day and decided to give me an awful taste of what it can offer.

I've been avoiding Julian since the situation happened. I can't face the shame and humiliation that comes with it. I purposely listen to doors opening and closing so I can choose the right moment to exit my room. I know his pattern well enough now to know what time he heads to work, what time he's home, and what time he enters his office. I feel like I'm living in this house without the homeowner's knowledge, trying anything I can to not be seen by him. I need a night of relaxation, away from this stupid house.

It's Sunday, and I had a perfect weekend with my family, filled with movies, cooking, and games nights. But leaving them made my heart ache. And to make matters worse, I now have to spend another five days in Julian's surroundings.

Returning back to the Gray Mansion is depressing, so I almost screamed in relief when I saw Curtis text me asking to have a history night with our old college friends. A night of quizzes and booze? I'd take a night sorting trash to get me out of this house.

I freshen up and get myself ready before Curtis picks me up. Wearing a long sleeve black turtleneck jumper, a checkered pencil skirt and black tights matches my lace up boots perfectly. I spritz my favorite vanilla perfume as Curtis informs me he's somewhat outside. His words not mine. I sent him my location pin, forgetting he has absolutely no idea why I'd be at a house that's not my own. Taking a deep sigh, I prepare myself to be grilled by him.

I take a peek outside my bedroom door to make sure the coast is clear before I try my hardest to walk quietly down this stupidly long corridor. Distant voices echo around me from Julian's home staff, and I'm thankful there's something to block the sound of my boots tapping on the floor.

I'm certain he's in his office, but I've been distracted while getting ready, so I can't be sure. I'm not avoiding him, I'm just too embarrassed to face him after he held my vibrator. Peering over the staircase, I don't see a single person. It's the perfect chance for me to get out without anyone asking questions. Not that I'm hiding where I'm going, I just don't feel like explaining why I'm escaping.

My phone buzzes in my pocket so I give it a quick glance, seeing Curtis is ringing me. I answer and hold the phone to my ear before saying hello, but I cut myself off mid word. My eyes widen at the noise, so I slap my hand over my mouth to shut myself up. So much for escaping unnoticed.

Panicking at my stupid mistake, I bolt for the door. With no time to glance around, I shut the door behind me with a little more force that I wanted. I can't stand around to wait for someone to investigate the loud bang, so I lightly jog down the driveway and punch in the pin to open the gate.

Freedom at last.

Or so I thought.

Curtis pulls up next to me in his beaten up Chevrolet and instantly kills the relief I thought I had.

"*What the hell* are you doing at Julian Gray's house?" He questions me like I've just committed murder.

Sighing, my tongue swipes my front teeth as I try to think of the right way to explain my situation. No words come, so I swing the car door open and hop in.

He doesn't drive away, so I glare at him, raising my eyebrows in expectancy.

He just shakes his head, looking more confused than I've ever seen before. "Explain."

If punching him would get him to drop the conversation, I totally would. But he'll just pester me with a black eye instead. "What do you think?" I question, giving him the same accusing tone he gave me.

"You're sleeping with him?!" Exasperated, he raised his eyebrows and turns his body, crossing his arms like an angry mother.

My instant reaction is to retreat, but then I realize I'll have to sleep with him sooner or later. "Worse," I say as I turn my body towards the front, breaking eye contact. "I'm marrying him."

Curtis's mouth moves in the corner of my eye, but no sound leaves his mouth. After a few seconds of composure, he finds his voice. "Claudia Harper Ibáñez, you better explain right now!"

"Drive first," I interrupt him before he can spit a selection of curse words at me. "Then I'll explain."

The car jolts into gear and we're speeding away faster than I'd like, but we're away from Julian's residence so I'm not mad. "And don't use the full name!" I call out. "It's mean."

"No, what's mean is not telling your best friend you're getting married!" I met Curtis at college a few years ago and we very quickly established we wouldn't step over the friendzone line. We just didn't click like that, but our friendship is faultless. I can always rely on him.

"It only happened last week!"

"Claud!"

"Stop interrupting me so I can explain!" I blurt, bringing Curtis's words to an abrupt stop. I can already feel my cheeks warming from the embarrassment. "His uncle owns my family's apartment block. They're putting the rent up and my family can't afford it. They can't afford anywhere else either. The only way to save my family is by marrying him."

Curtis's sigh releases some tension within the car, making me relax a little. "Claud, there must be another way." His hand reaches over and grasps mine, squeezing for reassurance.

"There isn't. It's for my family, not for me." I confirm, nodding my head as my defeat is obvious on my face. Distain grates at me as I'm reminded this is my life now. Letting out a deep sigh, I face Curtis. "Can we please not talk about this tonight? I need a night off from all things Julian."

Curtis nods and reaches for the center console to put the radio on, leaving me with my unwanted thoughts.

As we park, all bad thoughts are erased from my mind when I'm greeted with a bunch of history buffs, exactly like me. The 'Sunday History Quiz Night' is in full swing at The Coven which happens to be my favorite time of the week.

Curtis brings me a beer and we huddle around a small table with the rest of our friends. Every week we use the same name on our quiz, 'Brookside U' after our college, and every week we win.

My mind stays focused on every single question asked, swimming through the information I have stored in my brain to find the right answer. It's almost enough to keep my mind occupied enough for it to not wander.

Almost.

※ • ※ • ※ • ※

The most common known way to ease a hangover is aspirin, but the best way is to treat it before it becomes a hangover. Gatorade, electrolyte tablets, bread and a cold shower; an unusual mix to help you wake up feeling fresh after a few too many beers.

Because of my trusty combination that I mastered a few years ago, I never wake up feeling like my head is holding down a 10kg barbell. Instead, I'm waking up feeling refreshed, healthy and positive for work.

That was until I crossed paths with Julian this morning in the kitchen. Goodbye positivity, hello irritability. Just as I'm reminded of the embarrassment that happened over a week ago, Julian seems to be pretending it never happened.

The Julian who actually smiled during 'vibratorgate' is long gone. He's replaced with the Julian whose face isn't capable of emotion.

Perfect.

Grabbing a croissant laid out on the center table, I leave the room, not offering Julian a second glance. If he wants to pretend like we are strangers, then I will too.

It's not like this marriage is built on love, I don't expect lingering kisses or gentle touches, but being treated like I don't exist is worse than being hated. At least you're seen if you're loathed. You mean something to someone. You're a driving point in their emotions. Even that's better than being treated like a single leaf on a tree.

Insignificant.

But I can't expect anything more from him when he's just a puppet in my plan to save my parents.

Adrian waits outside the front door every morning for me, like clockwork, holding the car door of a very expensive black Alfa Romeo open. I sigh, unable to control my eye roll. Fuck the rich. They get everything they want at a click of their fingers, when there are people in Casamount who can't even afford to eat.

I make my daily debate of walking to work to make a point, but I'm already ten minutes late and my office is far away from Julian's home. Ignoring the fury burning in my stomach, I allow Adrian to take me to work, but I don't waste time making small talk. I load up my laptop and get to work.

"You're a perfect fit for Mr Gray." Adrian's sudden deep voice pulls my attention from an old historical building to his central mirror. I can see his green eyes studying me as he flicks his attention from the road over to me.

"How so?" I press, focusing my attention back on my laptop, acting like his comment didn't offend me a little.

"Workaholics," he chuckles lightly.

"We both love our jobs," I smile at Adrian. "At least I don't have to see him often." I semi-joke.

Adrian suddenly chokes on air, and I try not to laugh at his reaction. I don't know how much he knows about mine and Julian's business, but I know he wasn't expecting a response like that.

I have a full calendar this morning of building viewings and meeting clients, followed by an afternoon at the office attending a meeting and filling out paperwork. As far as Mondays go, they're pretty fun at my job when you enjoy what you do for a living. Always having a buddy system to go to viewings, because some people can't drive...oops. A friendly working environment, and I'm surrounded by people who love history. I can't think of anything better. Oh, and unlimited coffee, because I can't function without that.

Our afternoon meeting consists of monthly progress up-dates and donuts as we run over stats and changes within the company. Working for the city of Casamount means regular development check ins and a lot of business meetings with scary looking men, who look down on me because I'm a fe-male, but I'm confident enough to know what I'm doing. Plus, their shocked expressions when they realize I'm great at my job is worth it.

The circular table in the center of the room sits me and my other male coworkers as our boss, Rich, leads the meeting. I take in each word he says while I nibble on my sugar glazed donut, making sure not to spill any down my suit pants.

Our financial gains are shown in powerpoint form on the large electric screen, engrossing me fully. It's not until Rich suddenly stops talking that I pull my eyes away from the board and focus in on him, but his eyes are fixed on the door behind me.

Silence settles around the room as my coworkers dart their attention to the same door. My donut is half in my mouth as my teeth graze the sugar on top, tempting me to take a bite. But I don't. Instead, I slowly place my donut down on the paper plate in front of me and dust the sugar from my hands before turning towards the door, curious as to why the room has suddenly frozen in time.

Uncertainty pools in the pit of my stomach as confusion racks my body as brown eyes glare at me. I can feel my face warming with embarrassment, like a sudden flame against my cheeks.

"Julian?" I breathe out barely a whisper, my mind unable to form a coherent thought.

His eyes leave mine as they meet Rich's. "I need a word with my fiancée." His large index finger points at me, and like confusion and realization has morphed into one, my coworkers' eyes dart to my left ring finger.

Rich's gaze looks like he's been on a flight of straight turbulence as he tries to make sense of the news he's just been given. I don't share a lot of my personal life with my coworkers, but an engagement is something a person would share. Confused doesn't even begin to explain their reactions.

Rich offers a light nod to Julian while I rise to my feet, following him out of the room. I close the door lightly behind me as I direct him to my office across the hall, my anger brewing with every step I take. If audacity was a sport, this man would win an olympic gold medal.

Once we enter my shoebox sized office, he leans against my desk as he folds his arms, showing his tensed muscles. *I really wish he wouldn't do that.* I close the door behind me, unable to contain my irritation any longer.

"What are you doing? I'm at work!" I frown as I hold my arms up in frustration.

"No cheating." He states as he stands to his full height. "That's the agreement." His tone is abrupt and brutal, sending shivers all over my body.

My face scrunches up. "What?" I shake my head trying to make sense of what he's talking about.

"Who is he, Claudia?" He lowers his voice to a whisper as he takes a step towards me, cornering me.

"Who is who?" I shout, offended by what he's implying.

"The man you left with yesterday!" His chest pumps up and down as a visible vein twitches in his forehead. "And don't say he's just a friend! I saw you dancing with him at The Coven a couple weeks ago!"

My mouth falls open, unable to find the correct words to tell him he's wrong. He's wrong for showing up at my work, he's wrong for assuming I'm cheating, and he's wrong confronting me this way.

"Wait," I pause, trying to connect the dots. "How do you know this?" I question. I know his bedroom doesn't look out on the front of the house, just like mine.

He strokes a hand down his stubble as he backs up and leans against my desk again. "My PI sent me photos."

I'm speechless. I feel like gasoline has been poured over the lit match inside of me and I'm ready to explode. My freedom and privacy has been ripped from me like a bandaid from skin, leaving me exposed.

"You're having me followed!?" I spit with venom. The realization is so clear, it's like glass.

I don't wait for a response. "Get out." I demand.

"Claud-"

I don't let him finish. "Get out, now." I hiss through grit teeth. "We'll talk about this after work."

I don't wait for his protest. I open my office door and wait for him to leave. He silently refuses for a few seconds, but he finally comes to his senses and leaves without a word.

And I'm left with nothing but unanswered questions and deafening silence.

7

JULIAN

F uck my fucking life ten times over.

I don't expect much from people, that way you don't get disappointed. That's a lesson I learnt the hard way. If you expect things from people, you set yourself up for heartbreak. My emotions and relationships are kept locked in a steel chamber inside my heart after that day taught me a valuable lesson. The demons from my past won't give me the key to unlock it.

Once a contract is signed, I expect all parties to be committed. Not sneak off with a guy right after moving into my fucking home.

Betrayal is embarrassing.

I run my hands through my disheveled hair as my eyes bounce to my watch repetitively. Time passes by so fucking slow when you're waiting around. I've been sitting outside Claudia's office building for the past hour, waiting for her to finish. I'm missing valuable work hours and I'm paying Adrian to sit at home, instead of doing his fucking job. All because my anger burns like red hot liquid inside of me, driving me to get the answers I so desperately need.

My thumb taps my steering wheel as my body refuses to sit still. The past four hours I spent pacing my office at home, trying to calm myself down. To find an answer that would satisfy me, but nothing comes. My mind keeps telling me is she's seeing someone else and that makes me fucking livid.

Why? Because we're in a contract. A legally binding, legitimate, marriage contract. I don't give a fuck if she doesn't like me or if she's in love with someone else; she's with me and I expect loyalty from my future wife.

The photos my PI sent me are fresh in my mind. Images of Claudia and the other man invade me everywhere I look. She's smiling and laughing with him, looking genuinely happy. I'll never give her that now, purely out of spite. Not now she's broken the contract.

A sudden chill flows through my hands as my blood struggles to pump around my clenched fists. My steering wheel is straining as I squeeze and my vision turns crimson red. I tell my brain to stop thinking of her eyes closed and mouth open as she moans his name. I tell myself to stop thinking of him fucking her and making her come.

I can't fucking take it anymore.

Grabbing the car door handle and pulling it with so much force that it creaks, I step out of my parked car and pace towards Claudia's building. I enter the foyer, adamant on storming up the stairs to her floor, but something tells me to stop.

I don't know why I listen to my internal thoughts when they're the reason I'm standing in this building, but I stay rooted right where I am. I've already pissed Claudia off once today; if I want answers, I don't want to piss her off again. I need her somewhere I can question her without prying eyes and ears.

Time passes so fucking slow that I have to count how many times the elevator goes up and down to keep myself occupied. Seventy-six times until Claudia finally makes an appearance.

Her long, black hair flows down her back but a few stray pieces shape her face as her cheeks bloom a shade of pink. She carries her bag and a stack of papers as her heels click their way out of the elevator. Each step has equal rhythm as she squares her shoulders and takes in her surroundings. Her usually delicate features suddenly change the second her eyes land on me. Instead, she scowls and reverts her attention immediately, intent on walking past me like I don't exist.

"Where's Adrian?" She speaks, but doesn't stop to wait for a response.

"Having the afternoon off. You're coming with me." I walk beside her, my large strides matching her faster, short ones.

"I'd rather walk." She states plainly, looking at the oncoming foot traffic as we leave the building.

"Not going to happen." My tone is abrupt and demanding. There's no fucking way she's walking home. "You said we'd talk, so that's what we're going to do."

"I know you're used to having everything on your terms, but you can't just order me around." She finally turns her attention to me and I take in her twitching vein in her forehead.

Why is she being so goddamn difficult?

I use the only thing I have on her. "Fine. The marriage is off. You can move back home. You happy?"

Frowning looks cute on her.

Claudia's head shakes profusely and I know I've won. "No." She repeats it at least five times. "Fine. You can take me back to your house." A huff of disapproval leaves her bubblegum lips.

I notice she doesn't say our home. It feels like a jab to the stomach, but I don't correct her. It is my home and I'm not going to question why that statement feels wrong.

I head towards my car with her hot on my heels. I open the car door for her, but only because I want her secured inside of it, not because I feel like being a gentleman. I'm doing this for me, and for me only.

Dead air envelops the car, neither of us giving in and saying the first word. The journey to my home is an automatic response that doesn't need my mind to focus, leaving me to focus my attention on my thoughts. My mind is erratic as my patience runs thin, I focus on anything that can hold my attention. Car brands are the first thing I notice as I try to count how many different one's I see. Hyundai, Ford, Porsche.

Claudia.

Vanilla and peonies invade my nostrils as Claudia's presence hypnotizes me. There's no fucking way I can drive three more minutes home to question her. I need to do it now.

I turn into an abandoned car park and slam on the breaks, the car skidding to an abrupt stop as it throws my body forward slightly, jamming against the seatbelt. My gaze shoots to my right and instant discomfort consumes me when I notice my right arm placed along Claudia's chest. I tried to absorb the shock of the car throwing her forward by holding her against the chair subconsciously. I cringe at my body's actions, considering it forgot to check with my fucking brain before doing something so protective.

Heat burns my right arm, pulling my attention to look at the cause. My arm is still flush against Claudia's upper chest as she sits with her eyes wide open, staring at me like I'm not from this planet. You'd think she'd just seen a UFO the way her body is frozen in place, like if she moves, something terrifying will happen.

I jolt my hand away like it's under scalding water, focusing my eyes on anything that isn't five-foot-five and irritating.

"First, you storm into my work and humiliate me, which you had no right in doing, by the way! Second, you had me followed. And then you try to kill me. What's next?" Claudia's tone is demanding as she unbuckles her belt and turns her body towards me.

My face scrunches at her accusations. "I didn't try to kill you." I scowl at her, keeping my hands on the wheel.

"Oh, so you admit you humiliated me and was way out of line? Glad we can agree on something." She shakes her head and reverts her attention away from me.

"You want to talk about humiliation?" I question, unbuckling my seat belt and turning towards her. "How about seeing another man behind my back? That's pretty fucking humiliating, Claudia."

"What are you on about?" She throws her arms up, acting like I'm accusing her of something outrageous.

"You know exactly what I'm on about!" I barked, loading up the photo my PI sent me of Claudia in another man's car and showing it to her. "Does this refresh your memory?" I belittle her, knowing I've caught her in the act.

She squints at the photo as she studies it before her face turns to fury. "Are you serious? Please tell me you didn't ruin a perfect Monday because of this?" Her dainty hand flicks to my phone.

I scoff. "You think this is a joke, Claudia? You've broken the contract. This marriage is done."

"Julian," She argues, snatching the phone from my hands and deleting the photo. "He's a friend from college. We went to a quiz night with some friends at The Coven and he was dropping me home. Nothing happened."

A humorless laugh escapes my mouth as my nose twitches in irritation. It's always 'just a friend'. You don't have to be friends to fuck them, that's the whole point of one night stands.

I'm too busy thinking about a way to find out if this friend is what Claudia says he is, when Claudia's furious voice fills the silence in the car. "God, who do you think you are? Having me followed, invading my privacy. You have no right to do that!" She laughs, but there's no humor behind it. "What did you think I was going to do? Fuck someone else after I signed a contract? That's low, Julian. Even for you."

I don't like how her face turns in disgust as she looks at me. It feels like she's looking down on me, like I've accused her of something ridiculous. When, in fact, it's the only reasonable explanation.

"I don't know what happened to you," Claudia's tone turns softer, and I instantly know she's referring to a few months ago when I had my alcohol issue that the paps exposed. Good. You don't want to know, either. "And I know you have no reason to trust me, but I didn't scribble on a piece of paper for nothing, Julian. I stick to my word, and I need you to believe that, otherwise this marriage is going to be nothing but pain and misery, for both of us."

Is that the truth? I doubt it. So I make a mental note to do some homework on Curtis later. "Okay." I agree, accepting some sort of truce while I do my own research.

"Okay?" Claudia questions, almost shocked by my answer.

"I guess you're right." We didn't sign the contract for nothing.

Just as I think the conversation is done and civil, I hear Claudia ruffling down beside her. Glancing over, I frown as I see her hold my phone up to my face. "What are you doing?"

"Can you say that on camera? This is a once in a lifetime moment."

A huff escapes my lips as I shake my head, my cheeks lifting into a smile. It feels unfamiliar.

I haven't smiled in months. I haven't even used my cheek muscles to smile since *that* day.

"And no more following me." A stern finger is pointed at me from Claudia as her eyebrows raise in a steel glare.

Nodding, I agree.

Her attention floats around the car, lost in thought, but I keep my eyes on her as I silently observe. I didn't notice her freckles before, but they dot her face in a perfect constellation. Her cupid's bow is perfectly cut like she was hand designed by God himself and her eyes are so breathtakingly blue, they make the ocean look dull. Her aura glows so radiantly, even the sun would be jealous.

"Can I drive?"

My dazed spell is broken as Claudia's question gains my attention. She must pick up my uncertainty because she pushes out her bottom lip. It's sickening how cute it is.

"Please?" She presses, blinking her long, black lashes like a child.

Sighing, I nod. "Fine. One spin." I state firmly.

We swap seats and I put my seatbelt on. I watch as Claudia struggles with the stick and handbrake before jolting off, the car bouncing a few times before it moves smoothly. It begins jolting again and I can't help myself glare at her. Her driving is awful. No, it's worse than awful. It's fucking diabolical.

And then it hits me. "Do you even know how to drive?"

Staring at me like I've caught onto something top secret, Claudia's wide eye glare turns into a full blown, mischievous smile. "Nope."

I shake my head in disbelief.

This girl will be the death of me.

8

CLAUDIA

L iving in this house isn't getting worse which is a positive, but my favorite time of the week is when I get to go home for the weekend. I get to see my family and I'm not in the confines of all things Julian. It's the closest thing to comfort that I'll get.

My engagement ring slips off before I enter my parents home and doesn't slip back on until I leave. It's easier that way. They have a tight friendship group that believes all things social media is damaging to the mind, so I don't have to worry that they'll find out about my engagement through some gossip website.

Julian Gray comes with public exposure, and while I know I'm able to adapt to that kind of life to save my family, my parents would kill me if they found out what I was doing. I've only just gotten used to the dirty looks and whispered comments I catch people doing in front of me. I guess some of Casamount's finest females aren't happy that Casamount's most eligible bachelor is off the market.

They aren't the ones driving around in Julian's one-hundred and forty-four thousand dollar car. Without a license.

Ever since I took a spin in Julian's dreamy car the other night, things haven't been so tense between us. Sure, I still think he's an absolute douchebag and everything he does is infuriating, but we managed a conversation without arguing. That's an achievement. Even though he didn't apologize for his creepy stalker stunt he pulled and stormed into my workplace like he owns the building. But, progress is progress.

He's still an asshole, though.

A long day at the office preparing for a big upcoming meeting has left me exhausted. My eyes feel so heavy that coffee can't even save them. The only thing my body needs is some good food before I collapse onto my bed and sleep for twelve hours straight.

Adrian drops me home and I'm welcomed to the distant voices of Julian's staff echoing down the halls. I glance into the kitchen, checking to see what they're cooking, but no one is inside. I frown as I turn to make my way upstairs when I bump into something hard and rigid. Stumbling backwards, I accept my fate that I'm about to land flat on my ass, but two large hands grasp my arms and steady me.

Sage and citrus invades my nostrils, and I instantly know it's not Julian. I take in the large chest, muscular arms and expensive navy suit in front of me. As my eyes move upwards, I intake an involuntary gasp.

Holy shit.

A full but groomed beard, deep brown eyes and brunette hair scraped back into a bun. This man is *gorgeous.*

"Sorry," the man, who can only resemble a viking god, lifts his hands off my arms. I instantly feel the loss of warmth. I want them back there. "I wasn't looking where I was going. Are you okay?"

So, he apologizes and checks if I'm okay within ten seconds of meeting me. Julian could never.

I nod, shaking myself from the daze I was lost in. "I'm fine. My fault, I wasn't looking, either." I pause awkwardly, unsure on what to do. "I'm Claudia." My hand lifts, awaiting for a formal handshake.

Why am I handshaking?

"I'm Rhett." He returns the shake, firmly and secure. Like his muscles.

Stop looking at his muscles, Claud.

"And I'm interrupting." Julian's voice is somewhat patronizing as he strolls out of his office, standing next to Rhett as he looks down on me. "Are we sorted?" His attention turns to Rhett, acting like I'm no longer here.

"All good," Rhett nods. "I'll see myself out. It was nice meeting you, Claudia." His smile is charming as his eyes scream mischief.

I nod, somehow losing my voice I was using two seconds ago. Taking a few long strides towards the door, Rhett is gone, leaving me and Julian to stand in silence.

It takes me a few seconds to realize the voices I heard were Julian and Rhett discussing business and not Julian's staff. "Did the kitchen staff leave already?" I question, remembering they've never left this early before.

"They finish at eight. It's eight-thirty." Julian glances at his watch.

"It's eight-thirty?" I almost shout instead of talking at a normal level. Shaking my head, a sigh of disappointment leaves my lips.

"You can't tell the time?" Julian asks, and I'm sure he's trying to tell one of his amazing jokes. But when I look at him, he looks deadly serious. Almost concerned that he thinks I can't tell the time.

My face scrunches as my mouth pulls into a thin line. "Yes, I can tell the time! I'm just hungry and I'm dying for the spicy noodles that Caleb makes." My shoulders deflate as I come to the realization that I'm not getting my noodles tonight.

Julian seems to contemplate his next words as his eyes gaze at the floor. "We could get Thai takeout?"

Trying to act like a mature twenty-one year old and not buzzing off the walls at Julian's offer, I muster all composure I have and use it for my response. "Sounds good to me." I head into the living room and take a seat on Julian's stupidly big couch. The television plays a Natural History Museum documentary as the wall lights stay at a dim shade of cool white.

Julian's distant voice in the kitchen suddenly cuts out as he waltzes into the living room and places his phone down on the opposite end of the couch. "Foods ordered and Adrian has gone to collect it. It'll be here in ten." He pulls out a pack of cigarettes from his suit pants and puts one in his mouth, as he grabs a lighter from his breast pocket.

Leaving the room, Julian heads out the front door and stands outside. I see him through the living room window lighting his cigarette as amber glows with a lengthy inhale. I observe as he wraps his thumb and first finger around the cigarette and pulls it from his pink lips, blowing out a thick cloud of smoke.

His tie is loosened from his neck and his tousled hair is scraped back as usual. His suits must be tailor made because they always fit him perfectly. I don't know how he remains to look good at the end of the day when he works long hours.

It's infuriating and I want to hate him for it, considering I have dark circles and messy hair at the end of my work day.

But I can't say it's hate because I'd be lying.

A loud knock on the window pulls my attention as Julian stands with his cigarette between his lips and his arms up. Taking the cigarette between his finger and thumb, he mouths 'why are you staring' and I want to punch myself, because it's exactly what I was doing.

Scoffing, I shake my head. I mouth 'smoking kills' while putting my two fingers to my mouth and pulling them away, before moving a straight hand across my neck, acting out both words.

Julian's comeback is as blunt as him. A thumbs up as he mouths 'good'. I can't stop myself from breathing a laugh at his stupid response.

I mouth 'asshole' as I shake my head, but instead of reacting, he raises his eyebrows as a devilish smile appears.

Smiling looks good on him.

Rolling my eyes, I turn my attention to the television, trying my absolute hardest to ignore his distracting presence. I should be immersed in the documentary, considering it's my favorite thing to watch, but I can't look at him again, because I'm afraid I won't be able to pull my eyes away from him and his addictive smile.

I cringe at myself and my unusual introverted demeanor. Who am I?

Claudia Ibáñez. You know, the girl who definitely doesn't like Julian Gray and anything about him.

Adrian's return is more than welcomed as he passes the Thai boxes over to Julian. But Adrian leaves as Julian enters his home and brings the Thai into the living room. He places down the food on the central table and hands me some chopsticks. I waste no time picking up a box and tucking in. My stomach is immediately grateful for every swallow of noodles. Julian does the same as his fingers balance the chopsticks perfectly and hoists up some noodles before putting them into his mouth, giving them no time to go cold.

"No one is going to steal them, you know?" I joke, watching him as he puts more in, before he swallows the noodles he shoved in just before.

"Don't be so trusting," he glares at me. "You could be playing mind games so I slow down, just so you can take them."

I scoff at his weird thought process. "It doesn't make you weak if you're a trusting person. It makes you human."

Julian places his empty food container onto the table but keeps his chopsticks in his hand. "It makes you stupid. Humans have tendencies to please themselves, even if it means hurting someone they love. They'll always put their own needs above anyone else's."

A cloud of silence settles around us. I can't help but wonder what happened to him. I heard the rumors that he went off the rails, but I just assumed it was another rich boy identity crisis. But the way he speaks, his outlook on life, the way he's so reserved now. It's more than that.

He used to be the inspiration for all young boys wanting to succeed in life. He has money, his own business, a dreamy house. Women throwing themselves at him, no doubt. Though, that Julian isn't the one I'm looking at right now. This Julian has something he can't face. Something fearful and weighted, like a burden he doesn't want to confront. Instead, he's living in a constant loop of despair.

The conversation doesn't pick up after we sit in awkward silence, so I say the first thing that comes to my mind. "So, what are your parents like?"

Julian doesn't lift his eyes from his noodles. "Mom is an angel, Dad left before I was born."

Shit.

Shaking my head, I struggle to find the right words. "I'm so sorry."

"Don't be. I'm not. I can't miss someone I don't remember."

I'm patiently waiting for the ground to swallow me whole.

Not learning my lesson of breaking awkward silences with the first thing that comes to my mind, I speak again. "I've watched this documentary like ten times. I've always wanted to visit the Natural History Museum."

Julian's gaze is questioning as he frowns at me, but the corner of his lips lift. "Seriously?" He doesn't seem convinced.

"Mmhm," I nod. "Ever since I saw a documentary about it when I was little, I knew I needed to visit. Plus, all the historical buildings in London, I couldn't miss out on viewing those."

The clacking of Julian's chopsticks fill the quiet space between us as he gazes at me, lost in thought. I'm about to ask him why he's staring, like he asked me earlier, but his voice stops me.

"Intriguing, aren't you?" His tone is hushed and wary, like he's unsure he should have even said it.

It feels like a spotlight has been placed above me and an information leaflet is on display, filled with all information about me. I don't like feeling this exposed, and it feels like Julian can see right through me all of a sudden.

"Meaning what exactly?" My voice is barely above a whisper, and part of me didn't even want to ask, but I'm also desperate to know what he's thinking.

His head shakes as he looks away, shrugging with a smile on his face. "I've never met a girl who actually *enjoys* history. Most care about their clothing brands and astrology."

"You care about your clothing brands." I interrupt, my brows raised in correction.

"Yeah." Julian lightly chuckles as he nods accepting defeat, making me chuckle too.

"History is different." I admit. "There's always new things to learn and it's amazing to know the buildings I survey have seen a different lifetime. I like knowing I'm walking the same path as someone else a hundred years ago."

Calm quietness settles around us, and I can't help but want to ruin it.

"It's so much better than an investment firm." I roll my eyes and shake my head mockingly. "So many boring numbers."

"Yeah," Julian nods in a fake agreement. "Why would I want to do my job when I could stare at bricks all day?"

I suck in a gulp of air, fake offended by his comment. "You are such a dick!"

"That's a new one."

Glaring at him, I silently tell him not to make a kink comment, as I try my hardest to keep a smirk off my face.

Before he can consider a petty reply, I shove a mouthful of noodles in my mouth and swallow them.

"You dropped some."

My eyes gaze down to my stomach as I try to find the fallen noodle, but before my chopsticks can grasp it, Julian picks it up with his chopsticks and guides it towards my mouth. My stomach whirls as Julian shuffles down the couch, one arm resting on the back of the couch while his other guides his chopsticks towards my mouth, pulling towards me like a magnet.

The sudden closeness between us gives me whiplash as I try to make sense of what just happened. We actively stay away from each other, we share a mutual dislike towards each other, and we definitely don't feed each other food. But as Julian lifts my noodle up, I subconsciously open wide, allowing Julian to place the noodle inside my mouth as I chew on it.

The movement feels oddly intimate; something couples who are in love would do. Not us, who are marrying without the main component. But I can't shake the feeling of headiness. I feel drunk, like my brain can't make smart decisions anymore because Julian's thick scent of tobacco and cinnamon are leaving me in a daze.

It feels outer body.

I can see Julian closing the gap between us, my body reacting like an electric current as it buzzes with anticipation. I tell my body to react, to speak, to do anything, but I sit in a Julian induced trance. The only thing my mind can focus on right now are his plump lips, but my heart is also screaming something so loud, I just can't make sense of it.

His calloused hand grips my cheek, his thumb lightly brushing over my lips. His brown eyes drink me in, studying every part of my face, leaving me feeling like I'm under a microscope. My breathing becomes erratic, the painfully slow move leaves me frozen but impatient.

And like two live wires collide, his parted lips meet mine. A slow, sensual kiss swallows me, leaving me a puddle of mush on the floor. The gesture is so soft and gentle, two things Julian isn't. It leaves me wondering what this side of him is like. What's he like during sex? Is he kind and admiring? Or is he rough and demanding?

An image of Julian thrusting into a woman invades my mind as realization hits. Like a hammer has knocked some sense into me, my body jerks back, breaking the kiss and whatever hypnosis I was just under.

I suddenly feel claustrophobic from the intimacy. My body instantly fires into panic mode as I realize I allowed someone to touch me. Rising to my feet, I place the noodles down on the table, suddenly not hungry anymore. I take in Julian's confused stare as he backs away, staring up at me as his eyes plead for an explanation. He doesn't look angry. He looks hurt. That hits so much harder than I thought it would.

"I'm sorry," I shake my head, wiping my suddenly sweaty hands down my thighs. "I can't do this."

I don't give Julian a chance to question it as I speed walk to my bedroom, trying to leave all bad thoughts behind me. Shutting the door, I twist the lock and wiggle the handle to make sure it's safe and secure. My mind swarms with thoughts I don't want to entertain, each one getting louder than the one before.

I can't take this.

I'm safe. I'm safe. I'm safe.

I repeat those exact words over and over again, letting tears create pathways down my cheeks as I rock myself to sleep.

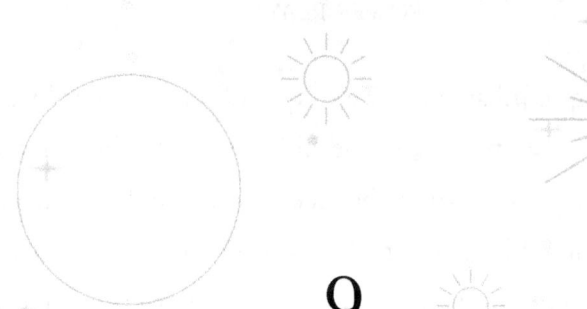

9

JULIAN

I ate takeout for this girl.

I fucking *hate* takeout.

It's full of additives and preservatives. I'd rather eat fucking stinging nettles, because at least they resemble a fucking vegetable instead of unhealthy, fatty food that tastes like cardboard.

And as quick as the moment came of us putting our loathing and differences aside, she ripped her lips away from mine. Instantly leaving me in despair from the loss of contact.

I don't know what possessed me in the moment to lean forward and kiss her perfect plump lips. It was like our differences had been stripped away and we were just left with pure sexual desire. Tension built a glass wall around me and every glance at her cracked the barrier. It felt like an other worldly experience, my mind yelling at me asking what the fuck I'm doing, while my heart controls my body, leaning me closer towards her.

The house feels unnervingly still, like no one lives here. Not only has Claudia been avoiding me for the past few days, but even my staff are acting like they have to be soundless. It's putting me on edge and I don't like it.

I've been spending longer days at the office, but even when I come home, Claudia hides in her room and doesn't leave until I head to work the next morning. I checked with Adrian, she's still going to work each day, just doing her fucking best to ignore me.

Is there anything I can do right?

I didn't have her followed or show up at her work. I made a very human decision and followed my gut, and now she's back to hating me. There's something else, but she's never going to tell me, considering that would require actual communication.

God forbid I try to kiss my fucking fiancée.

It's been a month since we got engaged, and it's been the most confusing month of my life. Even completing a rubix cube is easier than this. We'll never be lovers. We'll probably never even be friends, but I take our contract terms seriously. I'm not going to cheat on her, but I need to get laid before I explode with pure frustration.

I want her to talk to me and tell me what went wrong, but she's not exactly an open book, and I can't say I'm the most inviting person to speak to. I've never been one to entertain basic chit-chat. I'm only engaged in a conversation when it's something I want to talk about, like work. I guess you could say I'm selfish and self-centered, but I just don't want to waste time on things I get no satisfaction out of.

That's why mine and Claudia's conversation the other night took me by surprise. Speaking about her interests is no amusement to me. She doesn't entertain me and she's merely an agreement to make my mother happy. So why was I so engrossed in the conversation? She has such a delicate way of speaking, it's almost impossible to not hang on to every word she says.

I shouldn't be letting myself feel these things. I can't depend on people to not hurt me. I learnt from Adam that even the people close to you can still break your heart. I don't want to feel the pain he felt. It's just easier to not feel at all.

I scoff, shaking the thought from my mind. I've given her a few days to confront the kissing situation on her own terms, but she hasn't. I didn't jump to a conclusion and demand answers from her. I've given her time to think, but I'm also drowning in thoughts here too. I'm self sabotaging because she won't tell me what the issue is. I think I deserve to know, considering the ring on her finger.

The front door closing gets my attention as the sound of Claudia's heels echo throughout the foyer. My office door remains shut as I stand with my ear pushed up against it. I can make out Claudia speaking to the kitchen staff as she eats something, her mood seeming on the positive side. Almost like she doesn't give a fuck about the sudden halt between us.

She takes her time eating whatever the staff made her, probably some sort of spicy meal, before she makes her way upstairs. I slowly follow after her, making sure to keep quiet. She's unaware I'm home and she couldn't be more obvious to that knowledge as she leaves her bedroom door open and sings loudly. This isn't the avoiding Claudia I've seen the past few days. Which means, I'm the issue.

Irritance grates my nerves as my jaw clenches. I try to control my anger as my fists ball up and change to a shade of white. I don't push on further. Claudia shows more of herself when she's unaware I'm here, and I'm not wasting any more time waiting around for answers.

The constant fall of the shower water echoes from Claudia's open bedroom door, and I have to fight the urge to not send home all my staff. The thought of them seeing her fresh out the shower, her tanned skin wet and body exposed. I swear my molars nearly crack as my body tenses up.

I wait at the top of the stairs for the shower to stop running. Once she flicks off the taps, I see her walk past her doorway in nothing but a white towel covering her body. I pull my eyes away as my fingers and thumb pinch my bridge. Taking a deep breath of composure, I turn away from her bedroom. I'm not a creep, even if my body is screaming at me to take one more glance, I won't listen.

She changes into shorts and a t-shirt and lets her long hair fall down her back. I stay out of view as I catch glances of her lingering near her bedroom door. She seems on edge as she peeks down the long hallway, before she tiptoes along the long length.

I dart down the stairs, hiding outside my office as I try to keep an eye on Claudia, but stay invisible at the same time. I see her tanned legs stop at the top of the stairs, and I try to think of a plan to get back into my office silently before she descends, but my brows pinch together in confusion as Claudia doesn't walk down the stairs.

Instead, she carries on walking up the hallway towards the left wing. Why is she going towards my bedroom?

Curiosity gets the better of me as I once again tiptoe up the stairs to spy on my fiancée. Her demeanor is cautious as she constantly checks her surroundings, her body tense from the discomfort. I can hear her enter my room as my bedroom door opens with a creak, giving me the all clear to head down the hallway. I tread lightly as my eyes stay zoned in on my target. A million thoughts rush through my mind as I try to come to a conclusion. Why is she avoiding me, but inserting herself into my personal space when I'm not home? It makes no sense.

I shake all thoughts from my mind as I come face to face with my open bedroom door, and a curious Claudia stood with her back to me. Judging by her calm breathing, she doesn't know I'm here as she inspects a business folder I had next to my bed. That's confidential data, but I can't bring myself to take it from her delicate hands. It's more amusing to watch her. Her slow rise and fall of her shoulders, her whispered words as she reads out loud, her exposed legs and sapphire painted toes.

And then I remember how I've been left in the dark for the past few days, and my anger boils again.

Taking silent steps so I'm barely an inch from her back, I lower my mouth to her ear and I smirk the second she realizes I'm here, a hushed gasp sucked in through her rosy lips.

"This isn't your room Claudia. You're avoiding me, remember?" I provoke her, angling my body so she can't escape through the doorway. I dont miss her body jumping at the sound of my voice.

I can hear the thud of her raised heart rate. "I'm not avoiding you." Her whispers are barely convincing as she stays frozen on the spot. The lie just irritates me.

"Who are you trying to convince? I kiss you and you don't talk to me for four days. What did I do wrong this time?" I'm seething, my previous teasing tone suddenly gone.

She finally turns around, but her attention is looking around my room chaotically. "Get over yourself, Julian. It's not always about you!" Her accusation comes across venomous.

"How am I supposed to know that, Claudia? You've given me the silent treatment. I can only fill in the blanks myself if you won't help me."

"We don't even like each other!" Her voice is loud enough that it shocks her, her arms suddenly crossing over her chest.

"So, what?" I huff. "This is just a sexless marriage then, huh? You use me as a power play so you can get what you want out of this marriage, while I'm left with nothing?"

I swear I can see the anger change the color of her skin. Her eyes scream at me telling me to run while her mouth pulls into a thin line. "All of this because I stopped kissing you?" She scoffs, shaking her head in disapproval. Her eyes like glass as tears gather. "I don't trust you, Julian. I don't trust any man. You're all the same."

"What?" I recoil. "Same, how?" I interrupt her, confused, but she's so furious, I don't think she hears me.

"You take what you want with no consideration of others." Her tone turns quiet, almost shameful. Choking on her own words, she struggles to get her sentence out without her words breaking as she sucks in a breath. "And now I'm damaged. I can't trust anyone when it comes to intimacy."

Rage grips me as my vision turns red. Someone touched her without her consent, and now she feels like she's been ruined. All because of someone's selfish motives to put themselves first, and not worry about who they hurt in the process.

All emotions leave my body as fury drives me forward.

I think of the only way I know for her to trust me.

Claudia

The confession leaves my lips before my brain even has a chance to disapprove. I told him my deepest, darkest secret and now I feel numb again. Warm tears fall down my cheeks as a thick headache begins to gather above my eyes. I feel sick, weak and powerless. I just want to curl up and cry my pain into my pillow.

And to make matters worse, Julian left without saying a word.

I gulp down the lump in my throat as I try to think of a game plan or anything to get me back to the confines of my room. But Julian's reappearance in his bedroom makes me halt.

His face is stoic and determined and he has rope looped around his hands.

Shit.

Fear instantly swallows me whole as my mind convinces me the rope is for me. My fight or flight is triggered as my mind is erratic. I swear I'm about to go into cardiac arrest because my heart feels like it's pounding out of my chest.

This is what I was afraid of.

"It's not for you." Julian's voice is sharp, but not aggressive. Reassuring almost.

My teary eyes meet his restoring ones; something swimming in his brown irises that I can't quite place.

"It's for me. I want you to feel safe." His gaze pulls away from mine as he ties two solid knots onto his bed frame with hand loops. "You call the shots, Claudia."

I'm overcome with a tornado of emotions but I can't identify them all. I feel protected, heard, reassured. Overwhelmed that the ball is in my court. Scared at where this is going. But most of all, I feel hopeful that this marriage isn't doomed after all.

My voice refuses to speak up, so I just nod.

"I need you to use your words, Claud."

Claud.

And suddenly, the use of my childhood nickname makes me feel safe.

"Yes." I whisper.

A nod of confirmation is all Julian offers as he climbs onto his king size bed. I focus on his luxury bedding, the satin cream sheets probably costing more than my yearly paycheck.

Like he's done this multiple times before, Julian loops his hands into the ropes and tightens them, giving them a yank for extra confirmation. He lays fully clothed, but now his hands are out of use, I really am calling the shots.

A twinge of temptation tells me to leave him here restrained and restricted while I go to my room, but the heat pooling in my lower belly won't allow me to. I just need to get this out of my system. It'll be a one time thing.

The mattress dips slightly as I begin to climb over to Julian. My mind is like a playground as I overthink every single scenario. I inhale the cool air, and breathe out my anxiety as I focus only on the desire between my legs, the warmth curling around my body, awakening every nerve ending. I don't want to overthink this.

Chestnut brown eyes watch me curiously, not sinking down below my chin. It feels oddly reassuring.

Gulping, I rest on my knees as my hands find Julian's stubbled cheeks, slowly closing the gap between us. I'm unhurried as my lips meet his parted ones, sensually placing a delicate kiss onto Julian's.

But it's not enough. I need more.

I crave more.

Deepening the kiss, Julian follows my lead as his tongue enters my mouth. It's sultry and lustful as each new kiss is better than the last one. My core throbs as I give in to my needs.

Repositioning myself, I break the kiss to straddle him for a better angle. I waste no time crashing my lips to his as his erection throbs between my legs. I can't stop the moan escaping from my mouth, knowing I have the same affect on him as he does on me.

My hips automatically grind as I take in the sheer size of him beneath me. My clothes suddenly feel itchy and restricting, and I wonder why he isn't taking them off for me. Then I remember his hands are currently out of use.

I need physical contact. Touching, caressing, passion.

I need his hands.

Pulling our lips apart, Julian groans out loud as I'm automatically hit with the loss of contact. Forcing myself to hold in a whimper, I remind myself what I'm doing.

Reaching above Julian, I loosen the knots just enough so he can slide his hands out, allowing him the freedom.

"What are you doing?" He questions, perplexed as he eyes his free wrists.

"I trust you," I murmur, nodding my acceptance.

His barely a second long pause feels like a lifetime, but suddenly, I'm taken like a whirlwind as Julian spins me onto my back, propping himself above me.

"You tell me if you want to stop." His words hit me deep in my stomach. There's no way in hell I want to stop this. "I'm serious, Claudia. I often get a little," Julian pauses as he thinks of the right word. "Passionate during sex. If at any point you want me to stop, or if it gets too much, tell me, okay?"

"Okay." I nod. I'm ready for this.

Fire meets fire as we're engulfed into a flame of desire. Our lips crash together and an instant chemical reaction lights my nerves alive. My body is electric, each part of my skin crackling wherever Julian touches.

He sucks, licks and nibbles on my tongue, like a man starved.

Groaning at the material stopping our skin from touching, I reach for his buttons, undoing each painfully slow. Clearly, I'm not fast enough, because Julian removes his hands from my body and pulls his shirt open with force. The buttons flinging across the room and his shirt discarded on the floor.

My eyes almost roll to the back of my head at the sheer sight of him topless. Grooved abs, tanned skin, and muscles in places I didn't even know existed on a human body. His arms are solid as he holds himself above me.

Sculpted like a fucking god.

Panting, I make quick work of unbuckling his belt and suit pants, but my sight is black for a second. Like a flash of light, my T-shirt is whipped over my head and chucked out of sight, my shorts immediately after.

I feel exposed, but hot, wet kisses are placed down my jawline and neck as my panties dampen. I want them off.

"Fuck, you're such a stubborn little thing." Julian's insult should burn, but instead, it leaves me feeling more aroused.

"Please," I whimper, my embarrassment taken over by lust. "I can't wait."

Tsking, Julian shakes his head, a devilish smirk playing on his gorgeous face. "Needy girl."

Eyeing his erection before meeting his eyes, I give him a smug look. "I'm not the only one."

"Tell me if this is too much," I don't know what Julian is talking about before I'm flipped on my stomach, my legs in between his massive thighs as he holds my hands behind my back with one, large hand. "That pretty mouth of yours," his hand slowly caresses my bare back, stopping at my ass, "is what gets you into trouble."

A sharp pain lashes through me as heat blooms on my ass cheek.

He spanked me.

And I think I liked it.

"I was only telling the truth." I say, breathless. "More."

Another spank.

I bite my lip to mask the moan that escapes my lips. I can feel my thighs dampening, my core desperate for contact.

"The truth is trouble, Sunshine." He flips me back onto my back, and I notice the darkening of his eyes. They look hungry, and I'm the only meal in sight. "But there are other things I'd rather hear coming from you."

Anticipation eats at me as my heart pounds inside my chest like an out of beat drum. My clit throbs as Julian's knee presses against my core, and I instinctively grind on him. I need to be touched before I explode.

"Patience," Julian's teasing tone fires my irritation, but I don't get a chance to make a snarky remark as he rips my bra down the middle, letting it pool beneath me. My protest is on my lips but it's quickly swallowed as his hot mouth latches onto my erect nipple. Arching my back, I can't get enough of the electricity buzzing through me. A warm hand lightly pinches my other nipple, my vision blurring from the intense pleasure he's giving me.

Swapping nipples, his mouth latches onto the other as he pays just as much attention as he did before. The feeling is so fierce, I edge closer and closer to my orgasm.

I whimper, my hands getting lost in his dark locks as my legs open, begging for him to be inside of me. "Please, Julian. I need you inside me." I beg, not caring for my self preservation right now.

"Fuck," Julian groans, ripping his suit pants and boxer briefs off and discarding them with the rest of our clothes.

However big I thought he was under his pants, wasn't as big as he actually is. I gulp, sizing him up as I try to do some quick body anatomy math. There's no way in hell he's going to fit inside me.

Is it too late to run?

My blue panties are snatched off me so fast, the lace material leaves red marks down my thighs, but I'm still focusing on his size to care. I shake my head, pointing at him. "That's not going to fit." Saliva dampens my suddenly dry mouth.

Leaning forward, Julian places a slow, sensual kiss on my lips. "We'll make it fit."

Well, that settles that.

"Just one taste first, Sunshine." His breathy demand almost sends my eyes to the back of my head. I'm so overstimulated and I can't focus on anything. My mind is a cloud of pleasure.

Slow and sultry kisses are placed down my chest and stomach until Julian's hot breath stops above my pussy. Pure bliss takes over my body as his tongue licks me from my entrance to my clit. He releases a breathy moan and the vibrations are dangerous. "Fuck. I knew you'd be fucking perfect." He swirls my clit, adding a perfect amount of pressure that has my core pulsing. "Your pussy tastes like heaven, baby."

Fuck. I can't stop it from happening.

My body fires like a match chucked into gasoline and my orgasm thrashes through me, pure euphoria sweeping me away. My back arches, but Julian doesn't let me move. His hands cling to the undersides of my thighs, still flicking against my clit that I scream in pleasure.

The smile that appears on his face makes me want to hit him with his stupid expensive pillow. "That didn't take long." Julian's eyes look up at me, a sense of pride swimming in them.

"I've been out of practice, it wasn't you." I jab, teasing him knowing it'll bruise his ego.

"That mouth." He shakes his head, tsking. He rises to his knees, pumping himself a few times. "We'll put that to the test, shall we?" His tone is provoking as he lines his cock with my entrance.

I should've swallowed my words. I try mentally prepare myself for him, but nothing can prepare me for *that* size.

Anticipation fills me as he gathers the juices onto the head of his cock from my previous orgasm. He's teasing me and he knows it.

Whimpering, I look up at him with pleading eyes, but he doesn't fall for it. Instead, he just raises his brows as a knowing smile crosses his face.

I shake my head, knowing exactly what he's waiting for. "I'm not saying it."

"Say it." He provokes, his tone laced with temptation.

"No." I'm not giving in.

He shrugs, matter of factly. "Fine by me. I'll finish myself off." His right arm begins pumping his cock, his arm veins bulging and his mouth falling open.

Why does he have to look so good?

Shit.

I'm giving in.

"Please." I whisper, trying to hide the desperation in my voice.

"Considering you asked so nicely." He trails off like this is all on me.

A string of curse words are on the tip of my tongue, but they don't have a chance to leave my mouth as Julian thrusts into me.

Our mouths fall open as we gasp in unison, the action weirdly erotic.

I breathe through my body's adjustment to his size and he pauses, letting me get accustomed to him. He drops to his forearms painfully sluggish, his lips placing a gentle kiss on my lips. Edging down slightly, he places his hot mouth around my nipple, flicking it, making my pussy pulse.

I need his mouth on mine.

Grabbing his chin either side, I pull him upwards so his mouth is mere centimeters from mine. The heat from our breaths sends warm shivers down my spine as I'm hyper aware of every touch Julian imprints on my body. Our lips meet, creating fireworks between us.

Slowly, he thrusts in and out at a constant pace, watching my eyes for any signs of pain. But there is no pain, only mind controlling pleasure that makes me feel like I'm in a cloud of perfect bliss.

My hands find Julian's back as his hands find my hips, controlling his thrusts in perfect waves. He fucks like he's done this a hundred times before and perfected it as if he were graded on it.

He'd get an A star.

His pacing increases as he thrusts harder, the slap of our bodies meeting sounds lewd and salacious. The sounds escaping my lips only adding to the passionate scene we've created.

And just as I think this can't get any better, his thumb pad meets my clit as his cock hits my G-spot repeatedly, pushing me closer and closer to my orgasm.

"Fuck, Claud," he shakes his head, his eyes fluttering open and shut as he pants. "You feel so fucking good."

I whimper. My nails claw down his back, pure bliss driving my body.

A sudden heat meets my chest as Julian pushes himself flush against me, flipping us over in one swift movement. I mentally prepare myself to do all the work considering I'm now on top, but Julian's hands firmly grip my hips and hold me up slightly as he thrusts into me at impressive speed.

I can't focus. My mind is foggy and my nerves feel like they're on fire. Delicious shivers control me as my mind's only focus is what's happening between my legs.

"Look at us," Julian's voice is husky as beads of sweat gather on his forehead. I follow his eyes and notice he's looking at his cock entering my pussy, glistening with my juices. "We're a perfect fit."

"Julian," I beg, but I'm not sure what for. I could stay in this moment forever. My permanent drug fix.

"Fuck, say it again, baby."

I can't hold off any longer. My body is a volcano on the brink of eruption and nothing or no one can stop it from happening. My vision turns white as pure satisfaction shatters through me. I can't hold myself up as my pussy pulses, while Julian still fucks me ruthlessly.

"Julian!" I can't stop the word from slipping past my lips as I cry in pleasure, gripping onto nothing but air. Sweat coats my whole body, warming and cooling my skin at the same time as my body uncontrollably shakes.

Words leave Julian's mouth but I can't make sense of any of them as my ears throb, but it doesn't take me long to realize he's coming, too. His moans of pleasure are music to my ears, but what catches me off guard is him saying my name while he comes.

His convulsions are enough to knock me off balance as I fall on top of him as we both come down from our highs. Heavy panting is the only sound that fills the air as the scent of sex engulfs us, but the memory of tonight will last forever.

"It wasn't me, huh? Out of practice?" Julian's low, after sex voice pulls me from my sex crazed state.

I meet his eyes and roll mine, but I'm suddenly hit with a feeling deep in my gut that feels too much like fulfillness. Like my body is already craving its next fix of Julian Gray. I can't even entertain that thought.

"Well, we got it out of our systems. It doesn't need to happen again." I sit up, grasping the first piece of fabric I can get my hands on, which happens to be a silk bed scarf, and wrap it around my exposed body. I slowly rise to my feet, well aware of the warm liquid trailing down my thighs.

Julian's glance goes from satisfied to dislike in a split second as his relaxed brows suddenly dip. Is he really considering having sex more than once? No. I can't indulge in it. *We* can't indulge it.

He says nothing, so I make my way to exit his room, but Julian calling my name in his abrupt, bossy tone makes me pause at the doorway. "Your blue *friend* doesn't even come close to competition."

My eyes widen as I suck in a surprised breath.

I can't disagree because I'd be lying.

10

CLAUDIA

Is it bad to have a shot of vodka the second I wake up? I feel like I need it. I'm sore and achy in the best possible way, but I feel like I'm treading water in the unknown. No doubt last night will change mine and Julian's relationship, I just don't know how.

I don't like how unfamiliar this is for us. We detest each other, yet last night felt far from detest. We were simply existing in each other's space until last night, yet somehow, this feels weirder. Progress isn't even the right word for it. Instead, we've just slashed a divide between wrong and right, and now we have to manually patch it back up in the dark with no instruction manual.

All I needed to do was tolerate him and behave until the wedding so there wouldn't be any hiccups and my parents future would be secured. Now I'm treading on eggshells, scared I'll do something wrong before we tie the knot. Julian has already threatened to call the wedding off once. I can't allow him to use it as a power play against me again.

A deep growl rumbles in my stomach and I internally groan at my own hunger. I didn't want to leave my room today. I wanted to avoid Julian at all costs so I don't accidentally sleep with him, but I'm starting to feel dizzy and in desperate need of my morning eggs and coffee.

It's fine, Claudia. You'll make your usual banterous comment, he'll do the same, and it'll be fine.

Still wearing my satin pajamas, I lightly trail my way down the empty hallway and into the kitchen. Caleb and a few other kitchen staff occupy the room as my poached eggs and avocado toast are placed onto the breakfast bar, along with a fresh cup of coffee. I take that as my cue to take a seat and eat. My bare feet pad along the cold floor as I focus on my food.

Pulling the stool out so I can sit down, a high pitched squeak echoes throughout the room as gasps and winces follow. I look up to apologize, but the apology is knocked from my lungs as Julian stands leaning against the opposite counter, a mug to his lips and his phone in his free hand. His eyes meet mine but he doesn't utter a word. Instead, his eyes trail down the top half of my body, his throat bobbing as he swallows. And as if we are strangers, he places his half full cup of coffee on the counter and exits the room without saying a single word. No witty comment, no irritating huff, just deafening silence and painful ignorance.

I don't know what I was expecting, but it definitely wasn't that reaction. Hurt sinks deep into my stomach, making an unfamiliar ache wrap around my heart.

This isn't going back to what we are used to. This is completely different, and not in a good way.

My appetite is suddenly gone.

Uncertainty hits me. I don't know what this means. I shouldn't have given into the temptation last night. I thought it would be a one night thing, to get it out of our systems, and we'd go back to our mutual dislike. I should have just minded my business and secured my family's future by making it to the wedding, with no hiccups. But now, guilt threatens to rear its ugly head as I acknowledge my family's future could potentially be ruined. Because of me.

A black cloud of shame and regret stops above me. I made the choice willingly, so I have no one to blame, other than myself. But that doesn't stop me from pitying myself.

I want to turn my brain off.

Sliding off my stool, I leave my uneaten food behind me as I mope up the stairs and down the corridor. I shut my bedroom door shut behind me, instant flashbacks of last night assaulting my vision. I squeeze my eyes shut so hard, a headache threatens to appear. I slump into bed and wrap my duvet around me as I force my eyes to close. I want to sleep so my brain can't keep reminding me of what I've potentially ruined.

I toss and turn, restlessness engulfing me. My eyes squint as I grab my phone to check the time, realizing I must have slept at some point, considering I didn't hear the texts and calls from Curtis. It doesn't feel like my body had a break, but that's what a bad conscience does to you. It makes the suffering inescapable, even if you're unconscious.

I call him back.

"Hello?" I groan, rubbing my eyes to try to ease the headache.

"Get up, we're going out." His demanding tone tells me not to question him.

Frowning, I sit up. "How do you know I'm in bed?"

"Because I know your grumpy voice and you always try to sleep your bad moods away."

Dick.

"I don't feel like going out." I try to mask the pity lacing my voice.

"I'll drag you out of bed if you don't. Amalie will help me."

"Amalie is coming?" I'm pleasantly surprised. My best friend rarely hangs out with my history friends. They have different interests.

"Uh-huh. I'm picking you up in an hour so be ready." Curtis hangs up before I have a chance to refuse.

While my disappointment weighs me down and tells me to stay in bed, I'll take any chance I can to get out of this house and away from Julian. I shower and get dressed into a blue denim dress, a black long sleeved sweater and black tights. I scoop half of my long black hair into a butterfly clip and dab on some makeup to make me look less miserable. Spritzing on my favorite peony perfume and giving myself one last glance, I head for my bedroom door.

The house is silent and I take this as a good sign, meaning the house is empty. But I don't waste any time and speed-walk to the front door. My hand clasps the cool handle and relief washes over me, knowing I didn't bump into Julian.

Pulling the door open, a gust of wind fans me as I step outside as I taste freedom. But as karma likes to play dirty like the bitch it is, I bump into a hard chest as cinnamon assaults my nostrils. I don't even need to look up to know it's Julian.

I tell myself to not look up and just walk past him, but my eyes have a mind of their own as they meet his brown ones. I can't form words or even a smile, so I just stare like an idiot. Something similar to annoyance swirls deep in his eyes, but I don't wait around to find out what it is.

Breaking eye contact, I speed-walk to the gate and punch in the code like my life depends on it. The red light flashes back at me like it's laughing in my face for getting the code wrong. I curse under my breath, but compose myself and tap slower this time. The green light beams as the gate starts opening, and right on cue, Curtis pulls up with Amalie in the passenger seat. Hopping into the Chevy, I glance back one last time to see Julian stood on his doorstep, arms crossed, glaring at me.

Gulping, I tear my gaze away as I ignore the butterflies swirling in my stomach, trying to awaken the feelings I felt last night.

Sex on Fire by Kings of Leon thrum throughout the speakers inside The Coven as the dancefloor is a swarm of bodies grooving to the music. The scent of beer and fruity perfume wafts around the room as people sing in union. My friends have already secured us a table near the window so I hook my jacket onto a free chair and head for the bar. Amalie follows me and links my arm, her brown curls swinging with each step she takes.

We each order a beer but I quickly add on four tequila shots. The full shot glasses are placed in front of us and we take two each, the clear liquid burning as I down each in one gulp. I shake my head, trying to evict the sour taste from my mouth.

"Claud," Amalie calls over the music as she taps her card and pays for our drinks. "Curtis told me what's going on with you."

I glare at her, silently urging her not to go on, but she doesn't get the hint.

"You're seriously marrying Julian Gray? Are you sure you want to go through with this? I'm sure we can find another way-"

"There is no other way!" I interrupt her, but instantly swallow my frustration. I know it's not her fault and I shouldn't be taking this out on her. "I'm sorry," I shake my head. "I don't want to talk about him tonight. I just want to have fun and forget about everything."

Amalie nods in understanding as she links my arm and we walk towards our table. "Is he at least good in bed?" She eyes me, awaiting for an answer.

I shake my head and take a sigh of irritation, although I'm not sure if it's directed at Amalie or Julian. "Like you wouldn't believe." I whisper, hoping she doesn't hear, but her mouth falls open in shock. I point my finger at her, reminding her that Julian isn't the talk of this evening, making her shut her mouth and let the conversation slide.

We spend the evening catching up, dancing and singing until our throats hurt. I focus only on my friends, and any thoughts about a certain tall, dreamy man are expelled before they have time to sit.

Any man that grasps my hips or attempts to flirt with me, I flash them my ring before focusing back on Amalie. I'm not proud of how I got the ring on my finger, but I'm not a cheat, nor am I disrespectful. I have no interest in any other men and my loyalties lie with Julian, unfortunately. I'm not giving him ammunition to use against me and call off the engagement. He agreed to not have me followed anymore, but I stick to my word.

We play a game of limbo shots; a row of shots are lined up on a plank of wood and each person who successfully limbo's underneath it gets to take a shot. Me, Amalie and Curtis are the final three contenders like every other time we play this game. They make it too easy for us, so they changed the rules that we have to walk backwards under the limbo to make it more challenging.

First, Curtis is out after he bumps his chin on the plank, knocking a shot down him.

Me and Amalie are competing in an intense game before she accidentally loses her balance and falls flat on her ass.

"Winner!" I scream, jumping up and down as cheers erupt around the room. The winner's prize is downing the remaining shots on the plank, so I clear all four before dancing the night away.

Midnight rolls around fast as The Coven calls last drinks and people begin leaving. Time really does fly when you're having fun. Tonight has been a perfect distraction, but like all distractions, they just bide your time before you have to face the real issue.

Mine being Julian Gray.

The man I'll have to see in less than half an hour when I make it home.

11

CLAUDIA

I could be James Bond right now, sneaking into Julian's home and trying not to get caught. Except, James Bond is still calm and collected when he's been drinking alcohol. I could never have that self awareness, especially when the tequila is in charge right now.

Closing the door as silently as possible behind me, I wait until I hear the little click, before making my way to the kitchen. My eyes peek in Julian's office as subtle as the tequila will let me, and frown as I notice he's not there. I saw his car in the drive, so I know he's home somewhere. If he isn't in his office, he's in his room.

A wave of relief encompasses me as I realize I won't be crossing Julian's path this evening, and I don't need to worry about making any drunken mistakes.

I tiptoe into the kitchen, taking in the calm and silent state of the room. It's a completely different contrast compared to the mornings. The kitchen is the busiest place the second the clock hits seven in the morning. With cooks and cleaners darting around like they won't get paid if they're a second behind schedule; everything is on time and prepared with the utmost care.

Opening the fridge, a gust of cool air brushes my already warm cheeks, cooling them slightly. I fall in love with the feeling, desperately shutting and reopening the fridge door multiple times to feel the heavenly cool breeze. I debate sitting myself in the fridge for the blissful coldness, but my attention is suddenly locked onto the empanadas on the bottom shelf.

Wasting no time, I dive my hand in and grab the tray of the delicious food that reminds me of half my nationality. Deciding I'm going to sit down at the never used dining table, I stroll over and take a seat at the head of the table. My teeth sink into the pastry as I bring one to my mouth and begin chewing, noting the beef, potato, carrot and peas inside. I can't stop my eyes from closing and my voice box from releasing a moan of satisfaction. Empanadas are the best drunk food option a girl could choose from.

Before I realize it, six empanadas somehow work their way into my stomach. I'm tempted to go for more, but I don't know who they were made for and I don't want to eat all the goods. I think they'll notice some are missing, but hopefully they can be thankful I left them some. I could've gone hard and eaten them all.

Now I can no longer hear my chewing, I soak in the silence as I sip my bottle of water. I struggle to enjoy the peacefulness because I know it doesn't last long in this house. It turns into awkwardness and uncomfortably hiding in my room. But the complete quietness in the house tells me Julian is asleep, and because of that, I can relax, for now, without worrying I'll awkwardly bump into him.

I don't allow my brain to think about Julian, but it does anyway. Frowning, I try to not think about him naked. My cheeks blush at the thought, but then a cloud of misery hovers over me. I think about him not needing the deal anymore. Him discarding me like I'm nothing.

Ice cold water floods my throat as I gulp water, trying to distract my brain anyway I possibly can. To-do list, a closet organizing session, google giraffe CPR, but it's no help. My mind wants to think of him.

Releasing a frustrated sigh, I rise to my feet, not caring as the chair legs squeak along the marble floor. I'm irritated, tipsy and impatient. I just want the comfort of my bed and my vibrator, although nothing will ever please me as good as Julian.

I'm about to discard my empty water bottle when all my movements are frozen by one, intimidating stare.

Julian.

He stands to his full height in the doorway, his shirt sleeves rolled up halfway and his top button undone. His hair is disheveled, like he's been running his hand through it. His expression is stoic, but I know that look. He's frustrated and in need of something, and I fear I'm his target.

Brown eyes pin me like I'm bullseye and he starts pacing towards me. I take a step to the left, my heart pounding so loud, I can hear it in my temple. Julian mirrors me, stepping to his right. I'm silently thankful for the breakfast bar being in the center of the room, but I know it's a temporary barrier. I can't outrun him.

I notice Julian's fists clench, and I take another step to my left. Julian mirrors me, as expected, but I don't stop. I make it to the opposite end of the table I was just sitting at, but Julian has begun closing the gap between us. He's in close proximity now and for some reason, my fight doesn't want to play. My flight is the only thing that fires the adrenaline in my body.

I take in his muscular build and gorgeous face, noting how his presence makes me feel intoxicated by him. He may be a dick, but I haven't been able to stop thinking about how great the sex was. It's like a drug; telling my body to get its next fix, but my brain trying to be logical and not go back for more.

I deserve things that make me feel good.

We can both indulge in the sex and still disdain each other, right?

I snap back to the present, my mind tells me to run, to get away from Julian and his terrifying stare, but I remind myself he's no danger to me. I meant everything I said during sex, I trust him not to hurt me, but the fire inside of me tells me to enjoy being hunted like this.

Quickly weighing up my options, my eyes glance at my surroundings in my peripheral vision. I can't make it to a doorway without getting closer to Julian, so my only out is over the table I was peacefully sitting at five minutes ago.

I break the tension driven eye contact with Julian and hop over the table, trying to crawl myself along the slippery surface.

Fire burns in my belly as my only focus point is getting away from him, but I don't make it to the other side of the table.

His strong grip is around my ankles, pulling me towards him so I slide onto my back and down the table. I expect to see fury in his eyes, but when I meet his brown irises, I'm met with a fire burning inside them.

Desire.

Julian

Patience is something I severely lack, especially when all I can think about is Claudia fucking Ibáñez. At first, it was thinking about Claudia naked, then it was Claudia's tits bouncing as I fucked her, but now it's knowing Claudia has been keeping herself occupied with other men.

My cock is in control of my brain as I watch Claudia helplessly slide towards me, her hands attempting to grip the table with no avail. Her chest rises and falls with every panicked breath and her legs make a poor attempt to stay shut, but as my fingers slowly travel higher up her thighs, her muscles relax and her back arches into my touch.

I'm fucking starving and all I want to eat is her sweet pussy.

I followed the rules. I didn't have her followed. I did as I was told but what did I get out of it? Jealousy, impatience, hunger.

She's a fucking addiction.

It was hard to fight the temptation of calling my PI and sending him on an errand. My constant full whiskey glass kept my hands occupied and away from my phone.

I thought I was past the drinking.

A moment of weakness almost got the best of me, but luckily for me, my fingers clumsily tapped on the Instagram app instead of the call app. Claudia's best friend, Amalie, uploads her whole life on Instagram which worked in my favor. I saw Claudia dancing with Amalie, playing limbo and downing shots like it was a sport.

No evidence of men, but I can smell their cheap aftershave clinging to her. I want to fuck her so I'm on top, our naked bodies intertwined with each other, so the only scent that clings to her is mine.

Claudia still tries to pathetically crawl away, but my hands lock around her thighs, pulling her closer. I shove her denim dress up her body as her jumper follows. Rolling my fingers below her tights waistband, I yank them down, her thighs erupting in delicate goosebumps. Claudia wastes no time kicking off her boots and her tights, and my eyes focus on her sapphire lace panties wrapped around her curved hips.

I don't need to touch her to see her arousal.

My mouth is barely a centimeter from her pussy, my dreams and desires laying out in front of me like a three course meal.

"Tell me you want this," my voice is barely a whisper because I'm scared she's going to say no.

"I want this." Her breathy voice is laced with danger as she pleads for contact between us.

My cock springs to life at the knowledge nothing is stopping me from tasting her, I waste no time ripping her panties down her legs and feasting on what's mine.

My fiancée.

My wife.

Not yet. But I'm running out of patience not knowing why she's in this marriage. I need to know her pushing point, so I can keep her here forever.

I lapse at her core as I tongue her from entrance to clit, her lewd moans filling the air like an erotic song. Her hand finds my hair as she grasps and grinds herself into my face.

I can feel her orgasm pushing for release already, so I pull my mouth away from her. Claudia whimpers at the loss as she bites her bottom lip, sulking.

She's adorable.

Fuck, why do I want to give her what she wants? She's a means to an end.

My internal thoughts are on a constant loop, but I can't hear them over the sound of Claudia's moans as I suck on her clit. I push one finger inside of her, and then two as I finger fuck her, curling my fingers to hit her G-spot.

Her moans, whimpers and gasps are heavenly, and I decide at this exact moment that I can't live without them.

My name falls from her lips so delicately as she pulls my hair, grinding her pussy in my face. I welcome the burn on my scalp as my cock throbs, desperate to be inside of her.

Soft moans suddenly build to an eruption as Claudia's back arches, screaming a mix of my name and curse words as she comes on my fingers.

I don't stop finger fucking and eating her as she tries to pull away, her body squirming beneath me as she begs me to stop.

My fingers are soaked with her orgasm, only making my cock harder than before. If that's fucking possible. Bringing her juices to my mouth, I jolt my tongue out and lick off every drop, swallowing her taste, before plunging my fingers back inside of her.

Claudia's yelp fills the room as she sits up, her legs spread wide for me. Her hand finds my hair again, but this time she forcefully pushes my mouth to her pussy, her head falling back as I lap up each inch of her.

I'm swirling, sucking and flicking on her clit as my fingers find a constant pace in and out of her pussy. Lewd sounds fill the air, my dick desperate to be inside of her right now. "Fuck, Sunshine, you're so fucking wet."

Nothing but a sweet moan escapes her gorgeous lips.

"You taste so fucking good." I groan, not moving my mouth from her core to speak. "So fucking addictive."

I barely finish my sentence because Claudia is coming on my fingers, her legs shaking over my shoulders as her eyes squeeze shut. The words coming from her mouth aren't English and the pleasured sounds escaping her lips have changed from angelic to pure devilish, as she moans like a pornstar.

Claudia's orgasmic moans sound fucking euphoric.

Her body convulses and her arms give way as she falls flat on her back, her body still shaking.

If I fucked her now, I'd last approximately five seconds.

"On your knees." I demand, rising to my feet as she lazily looks at me with hooded eyes.

"Can't." She whimpers. "Body is too weak."

I see it as a challenge. I link my hands under her arms and she clings onto me, allowing me to lower her to her knees. She seems to know what's happening because her mouth opens and her tongue darts out, eyes looking up at me like mischief is her specialty.

"Hands behind your back."

She frowns at my command. "Don't you want me to-" she gestures to my painfully erect cock, before making an O shape with her hand and mouth, moving her hands forward and back.

I huff a laugh. "No. I'll embarrass myself if you touch me." I undo my pants and pull my boxers down so my cock springs free.

Claudia's eyes widen as she stares at my cock before looking at me and placing her hands behind her back.

"Good girl," I praise before taking myself in my hand and pumping. "Open your mouth."

Her tongue darts out as I pump faster, taking in each detail of her face. My mind flashes back to her writhing beneath me as I fucked her. Her whimpers as she came around my cock. Her moans as I ate her pussy. Her perfect tits bouncing with each thrust.

My nerves are electric as I feel my orgasm on edge, ready to explode. I want to be embarrassed that I barely lasted fifteen seconds, but I don't have time.

Thick ropes of come decorate Claudia's tongue and face as my nerve endings are electric. My eyes close as stars blur my vision, my body floating on a heavenly cloud of pure euphoria. My muscles weaken as my pacing gets sloppy as I ride my orgasm.

A sense of possessiveness encompasses me as I take a mental picture of Claudia covered in my cum.

This is how I like her. On her knees, doing what I tell her to.

"God," Claudia's brows rise and fall. "If that's you without me touching you," her eyes dart left and right as a smirk teases her lips. "I'm glad you saved yourself the embarrassment."

Shaking my head, I can't stop the laugh from escaping my lips. "Keep it up, Claudia."

"Or what? You gonna spank me?" Her eyes spark with a challenge.

Zipping my pants up, I sling her over my shoulder, ignoring her squeals and pleads to put her down, and take her up to my bedroom.

Sleep is the least of my worries because we spend the rest of the night in a bubble of erotic pleasure, fucking until the sun rises.

It feels like progress between us.

12

CLAUDIA

When something is going well for me, usually that means it's about to blow up in my face. I'm not exactly a luck magnet, so when a few things go to plan, it generally means misfortune is about to ruin my day.

I take this as a sign to secure what is a loose end, A.K.A, my marriage.

Guilt eats at me as I unwrap myself from a sleeping Julian and tiptoe out of his room. We're making progress, and it feels good to not have so much hatred building inside of me. But, that also means going behind his back makes me feel like a shitty person, which is what I'm doing right now.

We've fallen into a routine these past couple weeks. We go to work, come home and then we fuck like rabbits. Any conversation that would come under the 'personal' category, we avoid like the plague. Any other kind of conversations we do have, it's surprisingly positive, with the usual banter.

If I think too much about it, I fall into a hole of self-hatred. I should've never let it come to this. We shouldn't be reaching intimate highs together while disliking each other. It's a ticking time bomb ready to explode, and I need to be prepared for when that happens. That reality button is still flashing in the back of my mind, reminding me that this isn't permanent. Shit will go wrong, and I'm the one that will end up on the worse end of things.

I focus on my reasoning for being in this marriage as I get myself dressed and call Adrian round for an early morning trip. I repeat *my family, my family, my family* over and over again until the words get tangled, just so my mind doesn't think about a certain six-foot-one arrogant man.

Trees begin merging into one as I peer out the car window, my mind struggling to focus on one thought. Shame pulls me under its powerful waves as I consider the damage this will do. Just as improvements blossom between me and Julian, I go ahead and ruin it.

I don't want to hurt him, but I'm doing what I have to do. *This is the only way, Claud.*

My own words of reassurance do nothing to calm the nerves swirling in my stomach, but I push forward anyway.

My knuckles wrap on the familiar front door, and in less than five seconds, the door swings open, Edgar's eyes widening in surprise.

"Hi." I force a smile. "Can I come in, please?"

Opening the door wider, Edgar waves me inside.

I make my way to the dining room I'm familiar with and I ground myself by studying the paintings. I ignore the thuds of my heartbeat and focus on the reason I'm here.

"Miss Claudia, for what do I owe the pleasure?" Edgar sits at the head of the table dressed in slacks and a knitted jumper.

My lungs expand with a deep breath. "I need the wedding to be brought forward." I request sternly. I can't face him, because I don't want him to see the shame painted across my features.

"That eager to marry Julian, huh?" Edgar chuckles to himself, I can hear him pouring himself a glass of bourbon by the clank of the bottle. "The date's set, Claudia."

This time I turn to face him, my impatience driving my annoyance. "Well, I need a new date." Edgar's recoils at my tone, causing me to bite back any other words that attempt to escape my lips. "Please." Forcing my sweetest smile, I give him puppy dog eyes.

Edgar clears his throat, downs his drink and pours himself a new one. "Fine. Friday sound good?"

This time I recoil, my brows dropping as I stare at him, dumbfounded. Friday, as in four days away.

"What? Not quick enough for you, Miss Claudia?"

I *hate* it when he calls me that.

His throaty laugh snaps me back to business. "Is that your second glass or have you been drinking all morning?" I pry, trying to find a believable reason Edgar changed his mind so quickly.

"Second," he holds his glass up for confirmation. "It's a business plan, Claudia. My nephew is impulsive and sometimes I don't trust the choices he makes. I'm taking you up on your offer which also benefits me. If you're both married, I have no loose ends and all is well in the Gray family."

I nod, still unsure. "You don't want to know my reasoning?" I question. It puts me on edge at how unbothered Edgar is.

"Nope." His answer is blunt but not rude. "See you on Friday, Mrs Gray."

That was too easy. But I don't question it. I glance around the room to find an explanation for Edgar's chilled reaction; some powder or pills, but there's nothing.

Just the go ahead from Julian's uncle and my wedding in four days time.

This isn't how I imagined my wedding to go when I was five years old, planning the best day of my life.

13

JULIAN

One thing I've noticed about my Claudia is she will avoid a situation if she doesn't feel comfortable, instead of facing it head on.

She has spent the past four evenings working late, and has been starting earlier in the mornings, so she's only home to sleep. I've given her space, which is why I have to get this information from Adrian. He may be Claudia's driver, but his loyalties are still with me.

At first, I thought this Claudia was working late because she didn't like the good thing we have between us that neither of us want to address, but then uncertainty started to grip me as I feared I fucked up.

Then, my suspicions were confirmed when I received a text from Uncle Edgar this morning, informing me to be at the courthouse at ten in the morning, sharp.

My stomach drops as nausea chokes me.

There's only one reason I need to be at the courthouse.

There's no fucking way.

And judging by the way Claudia's been avoiding me...

No. She wouldn't do this behind my back.

Would she?

Rage burns my skin as I taste copper in my mouth. I don't realize I'm clenching my jaw until my teeth hurt, urging me to rub my jaw. I can't focus as red blinds my vision, my body desperate for pain. For punishment. For allowing myself to get into a situation like this.

Betrayal fucking hurts.

Just like it hurt Adam.

I warned myself, protected myself for months, but then I made the mistake of letting my guard down, and the only person I can blame is myself.

I shouldn't have trusted her. I shouldn't have expected her to be a good little wife. I shouldn't have let myself open my heart and give it to someone who has the power to crush it into tiny, painful shards.

I check myself in the mirror, trying to come up with some sort of explanation why this hurts so bad. I shouldn't be mad. In fact, I should be happy she's about to be tied to me forever. But we've built a wall of trust and loyalty these past couple weeks, just for her to smash a bulldozer through it and go behind my back. If she had just told me her plans, I would've understood, but now I feel disposable. Not worthy of her trust, her secrets, and her vulnerability. My mind keeps telling me anger is better than sadness and tears, which is why my body is a lit match, fuelled by treachery gasoline.

Blistering pain shoots up my fist as my knuckles meet my office wall, fury taking control of my thoughts.

The bottle of whiskey stares at me from across the room, urging me to gulp the bottle. To numb the unfamiliar pain I'm feeling.

Shaking my head, I storm out of my office and to my bedroom to keep my mind occupied.

I don't want to go through with this. Showing up to the courthouse shows I'm okay with this, and I'm fucking not. But I don't want to lose her either.

That thought alone rips me apart.

Sighing, I search my closet for a black tux suitable for a wedding and I get myself ready for my wedding day.

Torment and tragedy.

☀ • ☀ • ☀ • ☀

Pine wooden pillars surround the room with a judge's desk up front and pew seating from middle to back. The room itself is open and airy, but it feels dull and empty. Speckles of dust float around in the sunlight beams, giving the room little light. A USA flag is displayed on the back wall, the whites faded to a dusty cream.

Not a single person here to witness mine and Claudia's marriage other than Uncle Edgar, my mother and a judge, who all stand by the judge's desk. I didn't expect anyone else, but I can't stop the fury itching at my skin.

This is Claudia's power play and it hurts like a fucking bitch.

I refuse to make eye contact with both my mother and Edgar as I stand opposite the judge, by myself, as silence plays a loud song around us.

Claudia's fucking late to her own wedding.

Or she's not coming.

Irritance grinds on me, my fists clenching as my brain is on overdrive, begging for an instant release. I'm two seconds away from exploding and storming out of this room when the double entry doors open. Claudia speedwalks up the center aisle, dressed in a white suit and her hair sporting a bun, refusing to make eye contact with me. Her shoulders are closed and her cheeks blushed and a light shake is visible on her hands.

Good. I'm glad I'm not the only one hating this.

Stopping next to me, Claudia faces the judge who has now taken a seat on the judges stand. I can feel the heat radiating from Claudia's body as her arm lightly brushes mine. I want to grab her and push her against the wall, rip her clothes off and spank her until she gives me an explanation that'll satisfy me.

But I can't. I won't.

I tell my eyes to stay glued forward, but they betray me as I glance down at Claudia. "Glad I didn't file a missing persons report." I speak lowly, only loud enough for Claudia to hear.

"I'm sure Adrian kept you updated." Claudia tries to mask her shaking voice with confidence, but I see right through her. I can see the anxiety crawling up her skin.

"Adrian isn't my fiancée, Claudia. You are." I feel vulnerable showing her my weak side, knowing she'll probably use it against me sooner or later.

I see her throat bob, but Claudia doesn't reply. I think I'm seeing things, but a light tear drops from Claudia's lash line, landing on the floor below us. "I'm sorry." She whispers.

I want to comfort her. Ask her what's caused this sudden need to be married, but I don't want to press her for answers she's not ready to give.

Instead, I steel my spine and focus my attention forwards, trying to not get distracted by the five-foot-five mindfuck standing by my side.

Wedding days are supposed to be the happiest day of your life, yet here I am, so full of deception and animosity, with my teary eyed fiancée by my side. This wasn't how it was supposed to happen.

The judge reads her script so effortlessly, like she's done this a thousand times before. My face bunches up as curses threaten to leave my mouth every time she mentions 'love' or 'honor'. They're two things our marriage severely lacks and two things that definitely won't be present in the future.

We both lie through our teeth when the judge asks us to repeat our vows; it feels like we're spitting venom at each other, seeing who can be more deceiving yet convincing as our words burn like acid.

It's the performance of our lifetime.

We exchange rings that Edgar provided, sliding each ring onto each other's finger like we're madly in love. Looks are deceiving.

Glee beams from the judge's face as she releases a sigh of relief. She tucks her hands behind her back as her shoulders drop in relaxation. "You may now kiss the bride."

The anger, pain and betrayal are pushed to the back of my mind as I focus on the lust residing in my stomach. My hand finds the back of Claudia's neck, gripping her tightly as my other hand curves around her hip. Using her neck as a handle, I pull her closer and smash my lips against hers, letting my desire drive me.

It's heavy and passionate as our lips intertwine, my tongue entering her mouth. I savor her taste and I inhale her vanilla and peonies scent, taking in every inch of her as possible.

Claudia releases a small moan and her hands roam my body. I almost forget we have company, because I'm three seconds away from ripping off her clothes and fucking the fury out of me.

But then I'm reminded of how she's the instigator of this and I pull away, licking my lower lip to take in everything she's given me.

"Happy wedding day, Wife." I hiss, before adjusting my suit jacket and storming towards the door.

It hurts, being left in the dark with no explanation. I hope Claudia sees that now.

☼ • ☼ • ☼ • ☼

Edgar sends me a series of texts ranging from concerned to irritated, not getting the hint that I'm ignoring him. He wants an explanation. Something to justify my animosity. Because Edgar knows this marriage was an arrangement of convenience and not something that requires my stone heart to crack.

My mind is tunnel vision, only focused on finding out Claudia's requirement for this marriage so I can use it to my advantage. There's only one place I can find it and it requires keeping Edgar out of his own home.

I lean against my car, which is hidden at the back of the courthouse, and light up a cigarette. Inhaling a long drag, I shoot Edgar a text, asking if we can meet at the Enchantment Cuisine ASAP. He responds instantly, like I knew he would, informing me he's on his way.

I can't afford to waste any time, so I flick my half smoked cigarette into a puddle before hopping into my car and heading over to Edgar's home.

Trying to be light on my feet so I don't attract any attention, I head for the back door, avoiding Edgar's staff. For a man who's big on security, Edgar doesn't lock his doors. That's like putting a leash on a dog then letting it run off.

Fucking dumbass.

I could find my way around Edgar's mansion in my sleep. I use my knowledge of his home layout to my advantage and make my way to his office. The oak and white furniture gives a dated feel to the room. There's a musty scent lingering, probably from the old furniture Edgar's had for the past forty years. Everywhere in his home is modern except this room. Edgar doesn't even let his cleaning staff and personal assistant in here, which is why I need to hurry up. Any noise coming from this room when Edgar isn't home is an instant red flag, so I focus my attention on what I need.

I know he keeps important files in the bottom drawers of his bookcase, so I look there first. Folders with alphabetical letters on the front fall towards me as I flick through each one.

I check C first for contract, but I come up empty.

I move onto M for marriage, W for wedding, I for Ibáñez. Nothing.

Then I check G for Gray.

Two contracts, one signed by me and one signed by Claudia.

I fight the urge to grunt in success as relief washes through me like a strong wave. The anticipation tries to mount inside of me, but I don't give it a chance to fill me with anxiety. Instead, I pull the small wad of paper out and place the folder down.

The white paper fans me as I flick through, my eyes scanning at super speed, trying to find something that is relevant. It's all familiar as I remember the exact same words mentioned in my contract, but the section that mentions a sworn promise to my mother on mine, is different on Claudia's.

Examining each word slowly, my brain is trying to memorize the small paragraph that explains everything. It explains a lot; her home visits on weekends, why she wanted this marriage in the first place, why she's so goddamn loyal to everyone she loves.

She's in this marriage to save her family from the Gray's family success.

My uncle is using her as a chess piece in his game to tie up loose ends. His biggest one being me. He couldn't just do a nice thing and not put the Ibáñez's rent payments up. Instead, he manipulates everyone into being his puppets and uses them for his own pathetic game.

I scoff, frustration clawing at my throat as I face how blind I had been. I thought this was for my mother and her happiness.

And, Claudia. I shake my head, bitterly laughing at myself. Why didn't she tell me? Am I that bad of a person that she couldn't offer a small explanation for why she's gone behind my back and pushed the wedding forward?

She's deceived me by making me think she's sweet and caring, when she's an expert in deception. Her family's future is secured. She's a Gray, so her future is secured.

And me?

I'm hurt. Disappointed. Defeated.

I'm devastated that the one person I was beginning to trust and admire could stab me in the back and pour bleach on my open wounds.

14

CLAUDIA

Disconnected thoughts fire my erratic trepidation. I can't focus on anything, other than finding Julian. I need to explain before I vomit from my own self disgust.

I feel like I'm floating in the sea peacefully, but a sudden strong wave crashes over me and drags me under, enveloping me in a balloon of panic.

My fingers scratch at my throat, desperate for a gasp of air to cool my lungs. My surroundings start expanding as I shrink, a sudden doom clouding over me. It feels like I have alcohol in my eyes as they burn from my own warm tears. A painfully loud thrum echoes in my ear as my heart pounds painfully fast.

I feel alone and unsafe. Like the world can see my mistakes on display and are judging me for them. Like I've just made the worst decision by pulling the wedding forward and not telling Julian.

I didn't expect him to react the way he did. He seemed *mad*. Not the usual arrogant, uncaring asshole he usually is. Alarm bells clank in my ears the second he didn't say something petty. But what really made me feel regretful of my choices were the weight in his eyes. His brown eyes had changed to a miserable gray, like a rainy day that keeps you inside. I can't mistake the look of betrayal on his face. It makes my heart hurt just thinking about it.

I close my eyes and imagine his arms around me, his lips pressing delicate kisses to my forehead. It feels like clarity.

Realization slaps me in the face like a block of ice, forcing me to clutch my chest and take deep, slow breaths.

No, no no. Please, no.

I can't feel anything other than dislike towards him.

Don't panic, Claud. It'll pass.

But what if it doesn't?

My breathing spikes as panic once again swallows me whole. I can't deal with this shit right now. I need to find Julian and try and salvage whatever unspoken thing we have going on between us.

Me and Adrian have spent the past two hours circling around Casamount, trying to find a shred of evidence of Julian's location, but we're out of luck. "Let's head home, Adrian. I think we've exhausted our options for today." I slump against the backseats, resting my head on the cool window as droplets of condensation run down.

"Yes, Mrs Gray." Adrian confirms, pulling onto Casamount's busy roads.

"Please don't." I tell, almost choking the words out. "Claudia is fine." I guess he can't use 'Miss Ibáñez' anymore.

Adrian nods at my request and focuses back on the road. I don't miss the glances he's been shooting at me in the mirror all day. I don't blame him either; I've been acting a little unhinged today. How else is a girl supposed to act when she got married three hours ago and now her husband is missing? I take my bun down and grab a sapphire bow from my bag, clipping half my hair up and letting the rest fall down my back.

We've arrived at the Gray residence, but I can't even tell. The darkened sky matches the miserable feel of mine and Julian's home, with all the lights off inside the home and not a human in sight; it looks empty. *Like me.*

I have no hope Julian is here, so I plan on getting a bottle of water before heading to bed and wallowing in my own sadness.

Our home?

Slip of the tongue. This is Julian's home, and my presence here doesn't feel so welcome anymore.

Entering in the darkness, I feel around the foyer for the light. The click echoes throughout the large room as light brightens my surroundings. I slump my bag down and roll my shoulders to ease the thick tension weighing in them.

Opening the fridge door, my favorite cold breeze brushes my face, cooling my hot cheeks. I reach for the bottled water. I don't even give myself a chance to shut the fridge door before I'm unscrewing the lid and gulping the chilled liquid down my throat. Leaning my back against the door, I spin myself around, pushing the door closed in the process.

I force my brain to focus only on the water. I feel the icy feeling wash down my chest and into my stomach, creating a sloshing noise as I breathe in and out.

Inhaling and exhaling quickly as I catch my breath, I lower the bottle to the kitchen counter, but it doesn't land on the side. A loud crash echoes throughout the dark room, and my half full bottle is now in tiny shards, dotted around the floor.

I gasp, my hand finding my chest to feel my heartbeat. The foyer's light offers a few tiny shadows in the kitchen, making the slight movement against the back wall an eye catcher.

My thoughts are still incoherent as I try to figure out the best thing to do. Run? Fight? Scream? I glance around the poorly lit room for anything to defend myself. There are a few shards of glass that are big enough to hold, so I prepare my hand to grasp one if the figure moves.

Ice clinks in a glass across the room, snapping me back to the present, and now I'm three seconds away from panicking and running out of here like a lunatic. Adrian is nearby, I can run to him and ask for help. I nod, liking my own plan as I eye up the doorway.

"Don't move, Claudia. There's glass on the floor." Julian's gruff voice wraps around me like a restraint, freezing me in my movements. I can only make out his outline; he's sitting on a chair, one hand on his knee and the other holding a glass. No doubt it's whiskey.

I release a breath. "Where have you been?" I question, my panic starting to turn into exasperation. "I've been looking for you for hours."

He laughs, but it's not genuine. I can see his body outline rise to his feet as he places his glass down on the floor. He closes the gap between us in a few long strides, and I find myself looking up at him. My eyes naturally fall on the curve of his lips, his brown eyes and his large hands.

I gulp, my stomach swarming with butterflies as the heat from Julian's body burns into mine. His mouth is so close, I want to place my lips to his and let my lips do the apologizing, but the air is wooshed from my lungs before I can close the gap.

My eyes don't even register Julian bending slightly as his right arm is placed around the back of my thighs. In one swift movement, he lifts me up and slings me over his shoulder as he steps me away from the glass on the floor.

Heat pools between my legs as I feel Julian's strong grasp a few centimeters from my pussy. I wiggle, half trying to distract myself and half hoping his hand will slip. Anything with this man is addictive. I feel like I'm having withdrawals from just not being in his presence for the past few hours.

God, I'm a traitor to myself. I'm mad at him, yet my pussy had a mind of its own.

I didn't know how much I enjoyed spending time with Julian until the possibility of it never happening again arises.

Julian's grasp on my thigh tightens, forcing a moan to escape my lips. But before I can get my thoughts in order, I'm placed down on the other side of the breakfast bar. Julian leaves me and walks back over to the chair he was sitting at, grabbing his drink and pretending like I'm no longer in the room.

Forcing deep breaths to fill my lungs, I flick the lights on and compose myself. "Julian," he looks up at me with painful eyes and empties his glass of Whiskey. "Where have you been?"

"You want me to be honest?" He chuckles darkly, running a hand through his dark hair. "That's not our thing, is it, Wifey?"

Asshole. "What does that mean, exactly?" I spit, my arms crossing over my chest.

Julian stares at me with a fire burning inside his eyes, antagonizing me. He rises to his full height, not once breaking eye contact. He steps backwards, opens the back sliding doors, and pulls a pack of cigarettes from his breast pocket. He pulls one out, balancing it between his lips and lighting it with a dancing hot flame. Julian takes a long inhale before blowing out a thick cloud of smoke. "You aren't truthful, so I won't be."

I fight the urge to shout my point, clenching my fists and counting to five before I answer. "Why do you care?" I raise my voice, all composure draining from my body. "I moved the date forward by a couple weeks! What's the big issue?" My hands fling up as my shoulders shrug, bewilderment invading my mind.

"The big issue, Claudia," he takes a few steps forward, still puffing on his cigarette. "Is you didn't *tell* me. This affects both of us, yet you're the only one who can dictate what happens in this marriage. That's not fair." Julian shakes his head, his brows pulling together in what seems like despair.

Is he playing me? There's no way in hell Julian actually cares about this marriage and what happens between us. I don't believe that for a fucking second.

My feet are moving forward before they consult my brain first. "Now that's not fair." I shake my head, the familiar lump in my throat appearing once again. "I don't want to dictate this marriage. In fact, I didn't want this marriage at all!"

Julian breathes out a laugh, but he's not smiling. "You're not the only one who didn't choose this, but stop pretending it's been awful for you. I seem to remember you spending a lot of nights in my room after we spend the night fucking. I wasn't holding you hostage, Claud. You know you're in control when it comes to sex!"

"So, what?" I scoff. "This marriage is just sex to you? I wish it was that easy for me!"

Julian's shoulders tense, but his voice remains calm. "I'm not marrying you for a quick fuck, Claudia." His tongue glides across his teeth as he flicks the stubbed cigarette outside the backdoor. "If all I wanted was sex, I'd find that without a marriage contract." His index finger is placed under my chin, tilting my face upwards to look at him. He releases a deep breath, and the dull lighting makes his expression look hurt. "You used me to get what you wanted."

I shake my head and open my mouth to yell my disagreement, but Julian places his finger over my mouth. "You can't yell and expect to be heard, Sunshine." I gulp, his towering frame looking down on me, making me feel smaller and smaller by the second. "We are under a contract. Both parties get something out of said contract, which is fair. But you went ahead and altered the rules of the contract without discussing them with me." Julian's tone is bitter as he frowns his disappointment. "What did you think I was going to say, Claudia? No? You have gone behind my back and conferred with my fucking uncle about this! And you want to know the worst part? You didn't even fucking tell me. No call, no text, not even a fucking note." He scoffs, breaking eye contact as he looks off at the side, lost in thought. "In what fucking world would anyone be okay with that, Claudia? What's the point of a marriage if it's not truthful?" His tone is pained, and I have to blink away the tears on my lash line.

I've fucked up, I get it. But he's not exactly innocent either. Nothing about this marriage screams truthfulness. "Julian-"

He interrupts me before I can finish. "That ring on your finger is a symbol of partnership. It's a symbol of respect, honesty and not quitting when shit gets hard. Just because this between us started from a scribble on paper, it doesn't mean we can just give up. We have people relying on us."

That last line was enough to tip me over the edge. It's a grueling reminder of why I'm in this marriage. "People relying on you? Julian, you're a billionaire, you can pay off any problem you have! I don't have that choice, so I have to do stupid shit like get myself into a marriage and move a wedding forward!"

"No. Claudia, you secured your family's future two months ago! But you have so little trust in others that you only think about yourself and not the consequences your actions will cause!" It hurts because it's true. I was only thinking of my family when I pushed the wedding forward.

I'm about to answer back, when I realize he knows. He knows why I'm in this marriage.

It was never a secret, but it was a silent agreement between us both to not pry on each other's reasoning.

I shake my head, anguish lacing my voice. "Don't you see the burden I have on my shoulders? This is for my family, Julian! They'll be homeless if this marriage falls through." And then I'm reminded of who caused this. "This all started because of Edgar being greedy, my family are the ones who would be suffering. So, for your information, I actually have people relying on me, and I didn't see their future secured until we tied the knot. I had no other choice." I shouldn't, but I provoke him, edging close to him so our chests touch. "Some of us have real problems we have to face, Julian."

His laugh has no humor in it as he rubs his chin. "I'm a prick and I fucking know it, Claudia, but don't miscalculate the reason I'm in this marriage. I'm not letting anyone down, so this marriage is here to fucking stay." He pins me with a glare that radiates power and dominance.

I pull my mind back to the present, realizing we are not even on the same wavelength. We've had different paths in life which makes us different people.

I say the only thing I know that'll remind him of our current situation. "Julian, stop pretending like this is anything other than a business deal." The words burn the second they leave my mouth. I hate that it's the truth, but I need to face reality.

"Sorry if I find you hard to believe, Julian, but you have no concept of a real struggle in life-"

"I went off the rails six months ago." Julian interrupts.

My breath hitches in my throat, and I'm scared to breathe again in case he stops talking. My eyes are fixed on him, but he can barely look at me. Instead he looks around the room.

"I turned to alcohol and drugs. I lost myself completely. There was nothing my mother could do to help me so she just had to watch her only son give up." My mouth is agape, unsure on what to say, but Julian doesn't falter. Instead, he closes the small gap between our faces and places his hand on the back of my neck. In one swift movement, he yanks down my suit trousers and panties and flips me around so I'm bent over the breakfast bar. My body reacts to him like we're magnets. I can't hide my attraction, especially when I'm desperate for his touch.

His finger swipes my pussy, gathering my juices, causing a moan to escape my lips. I feel him line his cock with my entrance, painfully erect and ready to enter me. Pausing his movements, his mouth hovers next to my ear, his breath sending shivers down my spine. "Now, if we're comparing life struggles like dick sizes, I'm all for it, but we're nothing more than a business deal, like you said."

With one painful thrust, he bottoms out inside of me. A yelp of satisfaction mixed with shock escapes my lips as Julian grunts. His anger and pain is visible in how in fucks me. He grips my hips hard enough to leave bruises and his thrusts are vigorous. My nipples rub against my thin, cotton cami, painfully begging for Julian's touch. My mind is a cloud of bliss as I get lost in pleasure. All the problems we had before have suddenly vanished. It's just us; raw and real in the moment.

Lewd sounds and our moans fill the air as my orgasm builds inside of me, making my body numb and sensitive at the same time. I'm pushed to the edge as each thrust hits that spot inside me, my vision blurring and my body shaking.

Julian's lips gently graze my ear again, a swarm of shivers erupting all over my skin. His voice is low and intimidating, but I can barely focus on it as my high smacks into me.

"So, I guess all I'm here for is to feed you, fuck you and finance you. Isn't that right, Claudia?" Venom drips from his statement, poisoning me in the process.

Tear droplets burn my eyes as I'm floating on a cloud of euphoria, moaning and pleading for more. He fucks me through my orgasm, my body tingling in satisfaction, but everything else hurts. His words slashed a wound right over my heart, the blood flowing as fast as my orgasm. I'm trying to keep the tears back as Julian finishes, grunting and squeezing my hips.

I don't want to cry in front of him but those words hurt. We were more than that, but now, what's left of us? Two broken people with a relationship built on selfish reasons.

I can't be here with Julian anymore. He consumes me, and right now if he asked me to spend the night with him, I'd cave.

Shoving my way out of his cornered in position, I pull my pants up and jog out the kitchen. I grab my bag by the front door before running outside. My tears cloud my vision, but I blink fast so my tears fall. I dial Amalie, but she doesn't answer. Shooting her a text to meet me at The Coven, I hop inside Adrian's car, leaving Julian's home in the distance.

Julian's home.

Not ours.

15

CLAUDIA

The Coven is at its prime on a Friday evening, like expected. Drinks are flowing, hot songs are pumping through the speakers, and it's so busy in here that people are standing from the lack of seating. Bright stage lights constantly assault my eyes as they rotate, filling the room with a rainbow of colors.

The smell of beer invades my nostrils as I sit on a rusty stool at the bar. I place my hand on the countertop while I wait for the barman to come to me, but my hand is instantly lifted. My body shivers as the sticky texture has now been passed onto the palm of my hand. I hold in my gag and quickly pump the bottle of hand sanitizer sitting to my left into my palm, rubbing my hands together to remove whatever diseases I could've picked up.

Glancing at my phone aimlessly, I release a huff of defeat as I see no notifications. Amalie still hasn't text me back, leaving me to sit at the bar all by myself for the past half an hour. I order a beer while I wait, flicking through social media and counting the alcohol bottles behind the bar to waste time. One hundred and twenty-two, to be exact.

My eyes flick around the room, people watching and taking in my surroundings. I see a few familiar faces. College friends, Casamount locals and The Coven regulars. No Edgar, but I'm glad he's not here. I don't need a single reminder of the Gray family right now. I'm hoping a pretty face belonging to Amalie will appear through the crowd, but just as I have high hopes, my phone pings. Glancing immediately, my eyes skim over the text from Amalie.

> Sorry, can't come. Got a date with a hot doctor!

Sighing, I shove my phone back into my suit pocket and take a large gulp of beer. The grainy, sweet liquid leaves me feeling refreshed and tipsy. Amalie's love life is like watching the start of a hallmark movie. She met a guy at the park when his dog ran straight into her, knocking her off her feet and flat onto her ass. Since then, it's been wining and dining until the sun comes up.

I'm happy that she's happy, but I'm a little jealous, too. All Julian see's when he looks at me is a money grabber who is good enough to fuck. I don't want to be that person. I want to be *his* person. I want to actually mean something to him.

My own actions have left small holes in my heart, each trickling blood as my heart cries from the anguish. Each stupid mistake I made that got me to this point has left me in a pity party, and to top it off, my mind keeps repeating Julian's comment.

I guess all I'm here for is to feed you, fuck you and finance you.

Is that really what he thinks of me? Is that what he thinks of us? We're just coexisting and fucking when we need the release, just so he can keep my funds topped up?

I sigh. He only thinks that because I made him think that of me.

God, I'm my worst enemy.

I almost choke out a sob as tears burn my eyes, but I shove my glass to my lips, forcing myself to down my drink instead. Alcohol works as a perfect distraction. Until Julian invades my mind as I think about his words.

I turned to alcohol and drugs.

I wanted to pry and listen to every word that fell from his lips. I wanted to know his struggles and battles he faced in the dark while he was alone. I wanted to tell him I'm here for him, but I couldn't.

Instead, I ran away like I always do. I escape the situation and I fill in the blanks myself to fit my own agenda. I got really good at it, too. I'm a great people reader and I didn't need Julian to speak for me to be able to read him.

But I got it so painfully wrong.

I thought I knew Julian.

Julian Gray is the epitome of arrogant, selfish and blunt. He's a billionaire asshole who hates people and socializing. Except, that's not the real Julian.

Blue topaz catches my eye, my attention darting down to the rings on my finger. My engagement ring is now accompanied by my wedding band; golden with small, delicate diamonds filling the whole exterior. I'm sure the two rings on my finger cost more than a new house.

My brows shoot upwards as an idea invades my brain. If everything goes to shit, I could sell the rings to buy my parents a house. I could do that now; tell Julian I lost the rings and I won't be relying on Edgar to keep his word. A contract to me is a big deal, but a contract to someone who sees money as worthless as a rock, means absolutely nothing.

But I'd be running again, and I can't do that anymore. Anyway, this isn't about Edgar, it's about Julian. I can't lie to him again. Not after today. I don't know when the lines got blurred between us, when we went from enemies to seeing past each other's imperfections. I don't even know if he feels the same way, but the Julian I've seen the past couple weeks isn't the same Julian I met a couple months ago. There was emotion in his eyes. He cares enough to get angry and upset, and he felt comfortable enough to actually show it. That's not the Julian Gray the world knows, but it's the Julian Gray I know.

And I want to carry on getting to know him.

"Hey, sugar." Low, gruff and dangerous. My attention turns to my right as I see a large man sitting next to me, a killer smile plastered on his face. He looks like he's in his fifties, a large build with half fat, half muscle, salt and pepper hair with an ungroomed beard. His clothes look like they've been worn for the past six days and the smell radiating off him isn't much better.

I smile, not wanting to be rude, but I turn my attention away from him and back to the bar immediately.

"You're lookin' lonely." His thick southern accent vibrates my ear as he leans closer to talk to me.

I nod to the barman for another drink. He gives me a thumbs up as he begins pouring my beer. "I'm not lonely." I state, looking around for a person I know to save me. Internally groaning, I can't spot a single person. There were more than five options I could've chosen from earlier, why do they all have to disappear when a creepy man advances on me?

"You're alone." The twinkle in his eye makes me urge. I know what he's hinting at and there's no fucking way.

"Can't a girl come to a bar without getting hit on?" I snap, but smile condescendingly.

I don't like how his eyes trail up and down my body like I'm on display just for him. His tongue darts out as he licks his lips, his eyes hovering over my boobs a few seconds too long. "Not a girl like you," he uttered. "Too pretty." Winking, he orders a new drink at the bar.

Plastering a fake smile on my face, I nod in thanks before sipping my fresh drink the barmen delivered. I don't bother replying in hopes that he'll get the hint.

He doesn't.

"Seems to me like you need a big fella to take care of you." I'm almost blinded when he flashes a smile at me and his gold tooth catches in the light. I have to squint to save my eyes.

Lifting my left hand and wiggling my ring finger, I show off my two most expensive items. "I'm married."

Eyebrows shoot upwards, causing a bunch of wrinkles to form on his forehead. "You're a little young to be married, aren't you?"

I can't stop my eyes from squinting with dislike. "No." Bluntness slips from my tone without consulting my brain first. "When you're in love, age doesn't mean a thing." I try to save my rudeness, but I realize it sounds like I'm saying I'm into way older men, instead.

"So he's old? What's he called? Do I know him?"

His questions come faster than I can answer. I regret even speaking to this man. "Not old, just older than me. I doubt you know him. He's called Julian." Why am I even responding?

"Julian who?" Squinting, he rubs his chin like he's thinking long and hard of all the Julian's he's known.

He suddenly seems more lonely than creepy so I start feeling sorry for him. There's no harm in having a short conversation with him, right? "Julian Gray." I can't stop the lift of my cheeks when I say his name.

"Ohh!" He nods like he knows, but I don't think he does. "So you're Mrs Gray!"

"Mmhm." I agree, nodding as I sip my beer.

He leans forward slightly like he's letting me in on a secret. "Is he making you happy? You don't look happy."

I recoil, offended by his observation. Alright, I haven't had the best day, considering the reason I'm here, but it is my wedding day after all. I might not be ecstatic, but I'm definitely not unhappy. "Hey." I scold, pinning him with a deadly stare. "Don't speculate. He does make me happy."

"I could make you happy." He suddenly breathes in and grows a few inches, making me feel smaller than I already was.

"I'm happy with my husband, thank you." *My husband.* I shake the weirdness from my body and turn my attention to the front of the bar again, focusing on finishing my drink so I can get out of here.

"Liars get punished." His voice is low but demanding. He says it as a statement instead of a joke, and I'm suddenly feeling unsafe.

Panic tries to claw its way out of my body but I make it settle. This isn't bad, it's just a lonely old man who's out of practice at communicating with others. He just needs company. I'm in a bar full of people, nothing bad is going to happen.

I laugh at his remark and skim my surroundings, once again trying to pick out someone I know. There's no one other than the DJ, who is here on Sundays, and considering he barely speaks to his wife when she's here, he's not going to offer me any help.

It's okay, Claud. You're fine.

Inhaling a cool, deep breath and exhaling slowly, I ground myself.

Mr Creepy next to me seems to have eased off on getting my attention, as he sits facing the bar, one hand around his beer as he gets lost in the menu.

Half a beer left until I'm out of here and on my way home.

I make a mental script of all the things I want to tell Julian. I want to tell him I'm sorry for bottling everything up, for assuming all men are the same and doing things without him. I try to convince myself to tell him how I feel, but the thought itself makes me feel exposed. I'm laying myself in front of him like a cutting board and giving him the knife to wound me.

Sometimes we have to expose our interior for people to see our pure self.

Fogginess engulfs my brain with each sip of beer I take, each gulp leaving me more and more unsure. This beer never usually has this much of an effect on me. I feel drunk, so much so that my surroundings are starting to spin.

Dread weighs me down as I have a bad feeling something terrible is about to happen. I can feel my mind trying to slip out of consciousness and I can't hold on for much longer. I tell my mouth to scream, shout, do anything, but the message isn't getting through.

"Well, Claudia, I guess you're coming home with me after all." That gruff voice that seemed harmless five minutes ago whispers in my ear as an arm loops around my waist. He lifts me off my stool and practically drags me towards the back exit.

I'm confused why no one is helping me. Can't they see this isn't right? But no one is looking at us. Everyone is partying, drunk and having fun, not looking out for the girl who attends the bar alone.

And then I realize I never even told him my name.

I can't even hold myself up properly and my eyes are forcing themselves shut. I'm running out of time.

My right arm is already looped around the back of Mr Creepy's neck, so I unclip my sapphire blue bow from my hair and drop it on the floor. A piece of evidence in case anyone comes looking for me.

God, I hope someone comes looking for me.

Darkness is fighting for control as my body tries to win the losing battle. Everything feels too heavy. Signals are getting lost from my brain to my limbs, and it's a moment of acceptance. This is happening whether I want it to or not. He's going to take me and I can't stop him.

If I just stayed home with Julian, this wouldn't be happening.

A lone tear carves a path down my cheek as I think of my husband.

My grasp on consciousness is gone as my world turns dark and silent.

I'm so sorry, Julian.

16

JULIAN

A whole hour.

I spend a whole hour inside my mind, letting my thoughts run wild as it considers the worst case scenario. It's like chaos inside my head. I want to move forward, but Claudia takes residence inside my fucking brain, distracting my every thought. I want her to know that she fractured my stone heart.

To my surprise, I thought more of this marriage than she did. She's smart. She put her intentions on the front line and kept her feelings hidden. I, on the other hand, got caught in a Claudia daze. All it took was a five-foot-five Argentinian American woman to come into my life and turn it on it's fucking axis.

I stuck to my word, though. I settled down and got married, like I promised my mother. I had a future plan of building Claudia a home on my property, so we can live at the same residence, but not be in each other's presence. Now, I don't like that idea so much. The thought of not having her around here fills me with dread. I've grown to like the smell of her vanilla shampoo and I actually enjoy watching the historical channel with her. Whatever's on the screen may be boring as shit, but she's definitely not, and I enjoy watching her. Her big, intrigued eyes, her gentle gasps, her gorgeous smile. It's heaven in the form of a human.

I recoil. Pausing myself as I try to understand where these feelings are coming from and why they feel so vulnerable.

She played me to get what she wanted.

That should be enough to deter me from her forever, but I have a pulling feeling inside my heart, directing me towards her.

I scoff. There's no fucking way I'm going there.

I'm not chasing after her when she's the reason today went so fucking wrong in the first place.

I said some things I regret, and I'm sure she did too. I want to say that universal word that makes everything okay and excuses your actions, but where's the middle ground? I go and apologize for all the bad things I said, but what if it's not enough?

I guess that's the thing about this weird, adoration feeling inside my heart. It's selflessness.

You don't care if you're the one getting burned in the fire, as long as the person you love is safe from the flame.

Fuck it, I'm going to find her.

Hopping into my Merc like time is crucial, I flick the key and press the gas pedal. High pitch squeals come from my tires as my car struggles with the sudden speed request, but I don't let up. Jolting backwards in my leather seat, I pull out of my driveway and head to the one place I know Claudia will be.

The Coven.

I don't wait for a parking space to hit my line of sight. Instead, I pull up on the curb outside the bar, not giving a fuck I could be ticketed for this.

I'm quickly deterred by the amount of people queuing outside, reminding me it's Friday. Cursing under my breath, I skip the queue and stop in front of a large male with a security shirt on. Holding up a few hundred dollar bills between my fingers, I nod towards the entrance doors. "My wife is inside, I need to find her."

With a delayed reaction and a nod of confirmation, the barrier is pulled to the side and I'm let through. I can hear groans and words of disapproval from the lengthy queue behind me.

Raising my voice loud enough so they can hear, I stand just inside The Coven doors. "It's nice and warm here, I'll have a beer for you guys."

A laugh slips my lip as I'm hurled a selection of curse words and insults. It was worth it.

The Coven is the visual representation of an old school bus. It's got ugly patterns decorating the inside and it smells like it's a hundred years old. I don't know why Claudia is a regular here. Or my uncle for that matter.

I glance around the busy room, trying to find the familiar black hair. There are men too old to be here, women acting a bit wild now they aren't in the company of their husbands, and younger crowds happy to be inside somewhere they're not old enough for. But no Claudia.

I try to search for Amalie or Claudia's history friends, but I can't see anyone. My eyes dart left to right, up and down, but

I'm completely out of luck. Did I go to the wrong location? I was certain she would be here.

Maybe I don't know her as well as I thought I did.

I shove the ache inside my chest to the back of my mind as I focus on the reason I'm here. I don't have fucking time for a pity party.

Shoving my way to the bar, I maneuver my way through the swarm of people. People are annoying enough when they're sober, but when people are drunk? That's the most irritating shit to deal with when you're sober yourself.

A young barman occupies the bar alone, I figure he's new considering he doesn't even look the legal age to work here. "Buddy!" I shout, nodding my head at him to get his attention. I decided on a friendly approach at the last second, but cringed the second the word 'buddy' left my lips.

The barman leans over towards me, trying to make sure he can hear me over the loud, pumping music. "Have you seen my wife?" His brows pull together in confusion, unsure on where the conversation is going. "She's in a white suit." I add on, and his expression instantly changes.

His eyebrows soften and he nods, turning his head to the right of the bar, but looking confused when no one is sitting there. "She was right there with some guy!" He points at the empty seats, but I can't hear the rest of what he says. My ears are burning hot with rage as my heart pumps pure fury around my body.

Some fucking guy.

My right foot is in front of my left, heading towards the back door, but a sudden crunch under my foot pauses me in my tracks. Lifting my shoe, I see a sapphire hair bow, now broken. Picking it up and grasping it in my hand, I study it for a few more seconds, but I don't need long to know it's Claudia's. It's the exact same one she wears at least three times a week.

That girl cherishes her hair bow collection like they're her first born child. There's no way she's dropping one and not realizing it.

I don't like the feeling that sits deep in my stomach. Anxiety mixed with concern makes a dangerous concoction, as they drive my need to find Claudia faster than a race car. The back exit door opens with a thud as my eyes scan the alleyway in almost darkness. A little light from the street lamp is enough to make out slight movements, but I rely more on my ears to hear for anything concerning.

Grunts and pants come from my left, but all I can see are large dumpsters. I don't waste time wondering what the noise is, instead, I pace over, squinting to make sense of what I can't see.

All I can spot is a large body, crouching forward, fiddling with something on the floor. I'm guessing it's a man from the body build and the sounds coming from their mouth. I assume it's drugs or something harmless, but then I notice a white sleeve from underneath the man's legs.

The color is all I need to see to know who it is.

All coherent thoughts have vanished from my brain, and in their place is pure, animalistic rage. Everything is red, warning my surroundings of the danger building inside of me. I taste copper in my mouth from clenching my jaw so hard, my gum bleeds. My breathing is fast and deep as I try to keep myself calm, but my clenched fists and tense shoulders are a warning of what's about to come.

He doesn't even hear me standing directly behind him, he's so engrossed in something I can't see, and I'm not sure I want to.

My right hand grips his shoulder, instantly making him flinch and gasp. I yank him backwards so he falls flat on his ass, but he's no longer a single thought in my mind.

The only thought occupying my mind right now is the vision of my wife passed out on the floor, clothes ripped and dirtied, clinging onto her body as they keep her protected. She's always responsible. Claudia would never allow herself to get this drunk. He forced himself onto her.

Onto a Gray.

He deserves to be tortured for that.

A string of words leave his mouth as he tries to stand his drunk ass up, but he isn't leaving my sight. Balling my right fist up, I swing and connect with his cheekbone, releasing every ounce of anger into him. He hit the floor with a loud thud, his consciousness long gone.

"Claud, baby." My eyes hover over her body, checking for any injuries. She stirs awake, but whatever fucking drug he's given her has her buzzed. She can't even count to five right now.

Dropping to my knees, I brush stray hair from her face as I rub the pad of my thumb across her delicate cheek. It's bruised and cut, the sight alone strangling my heart. Placing a hand under her back, I pull her onto my lap, cradling her. "I'm here, Sunshine. I'm sorry I didn't run after you when you left. This shouldn't have happened." The confession slips from my lips so easily, knowing she can't hear.

I can't leave her out here, but I'm not done with him either.

Fishing my phone from my pocket, I dial Rhett. He takes his fucking time to answer, but as soon as he does, I tell him to get his ass down here ASAP. I don't know how long this guy will be knocked out for, so I give Rhett a quick rundown of the important situation.

Shoving off my jacket, I place it on top of Claudia, welcoming the cool breeze that caresses my red hot skin. Wrapping my arms under Claudia's thighs and back, I scoop her up and snuggle her into me, desperately wanting her to give me all of her pain.

I turn to head towards my car, but I really don't want this fucker getting away with this, so I abruptly turn, placing a strong kick into the back of his head. His limp body jolts, but remains still after the initial impact. I pray it keeps him knocked out long enough for Rhett to arrive.

My eyes fall to Claudia as I run back to my car. Each delicate feature is a gift from the angels above. There's not a single part of her that isn't perfect. An imperfection is a myth when it comes to Claudia, even the gods are jealous of her.

Claudia Gray is ethereal. And Claudia Gray is mine.

My heart squeezes each second I look at her. My one purpose as her husband is to protect her from harm, and I couldn't even fucking do that.

Placing her into the passenger side gently, I strap her in to drive us home at illegal speed. I'd break twenty laws if it means keeping her safe. My impatience causes me to be jittery, tapping the steering wheel and unable to focus on anything.

My central consol notifies me I have an incoming call. I answer, and instantly relax when I hear Rhett's voice. "Got him." Two words fill me with relief and rage at the same time.

"Nice work." I switch lanes, zeroing in on the Gray residence. "I'll meet you at the warehouse in ten."

Punching in the code, the gates open and I drive in. I park my car in my usual garage spot before climbing out and unclipping Claudia. She's still unconscious, so I put her in the one place I want her to feel safe.

My hands grasp her thighs and back and I scoop her into my front, counting the slow rise and fall of her chest. Clutching her close, I carry her up the stairs and down the hall to my bedroom. Memories of our last time in this room together invade my mind, but I push them away. I'll be forever punished by Satan if I get a boner right fucking now.

Gently placing Claudia down in the center of the bed, I brush her hair from her face and gaze at the blessing in front of me. She's really saved me from my demons.

I glance at her ripped clothing and immediately start undressing her. There's no way in hell I'm letting her stay in clothes that some prick has touched. I make a mental note to bath her once she's awake to remove any touch he left. She needs a soothing touch and I need to be it.

Placing one of my T-shirt's over her head, I tuck her arms in and pull the duvet up to her chin.

Fucking adorable.

I soak in her image, mentally painting an invaluable picture of her in my head. I watch her chest rise and fall with each breath. But I fight the urge to pull her into me. If I have her in my grasp, I'll never let go, but I need to sort this fucker out.

My text tone reminds me Rhett is waiting for me, so I rise to my feet and pull my phone out my pocket, but a light, hushed voice grasps my attention.

"I'm sorry." Claudia's voice is raspy and barely audible as her eyes barely flick open.

"Shh. Go to sleep, baby." I take a deep breath and place a gentle kiss on her forehead before rising to my full height.

Her hand is holding mine lightly, giving it a squeeze. "What's going to happen to him?"

"He'll get what he deserves."

Violent images flash in my mind as my sole focus is justice.

No one touches my wife and goes unpunished.

His regret will run deeper than the ocean.

17

JULIAN

Justice is the legal way of saying people get what they deserve, and I'm more than happy to give this man his fate without going through the system. They'd be too kind to him. Let him off with no jail time.

He'll be begging for death by the time I'm finished with him, and I wouldn't dare grant him that mercy.

I have Magda under strict instructions to check on Claudia every ten minutes to check she's okay and if she needs anything. I want to be at home in bed with her, holding her close to my chest and kissing the bad memories away.

But husband duties call.

The warehouse I'm meeting Rhett at is on the outskirts of Casamount and is surrounded by nothing except fields. It's secluded and doesn't attract any human activity, therefore, it's the perfect place to torture someone.

I spot Rhett's car outside as I pull up and park next to him, before making my way inside. The scent of copper and hay invades my nostrils as I take in the abandoned warehouse. It's basically empty, bar the few stacks of hay that have been left for years. They're stale and musty, but were the perfect seats for me and Rhett when we were sneaking out at midnight at fourteen years old.

There's barely any light inside, other than a few automated emergency lights attached to the metal sheet ceiling, adding a tinge of danger to the chipped red painted walls. It's enough to see my close surroundings and it also protects the warehouse from standing out.

"He's out cold." Rhett utters huskily. He points towards the other end of the warehouse, before nodding in that direction.

I take the lead and head towards the opposite end, each of our footsteps echoing with each tread.

A distant figure comes into view as we zero in on our target. He's sitting on a rusty chair that is on the brink of collapse, with his arms tied behind his back and his ankles tied to the chair legs.

A thick strip of duct tape is placed over his mouth; I'm guessing he was a screamer on his way over here that Rhett had to take matters into his own hands. Finding a creased corner, I pinch it between my forefinger and thumb and rip it from his face. I hear skin tearing off his lips, evidence of the damage on the tape. Small specks of crimson appear on his lips, but he's still completely out of it.

The thought of him resting peacefully only enrages me more.

I turn to the makeshift table behind me; a hay bale with a cream sheet placed on top, with a selection of metal instruments laid out neatly. Knives, pliers, scissors, a dental drill, accompanied with a tub of salt and a bottle of bleach. Choosing a gutting hunting knife, I inspect the sharpness before turning around.

Pacing slowly around the occupied chair, I stand behind the unconscious male, shoving his head forward to check he's still out of it. Lifting my right arm up, I plunge the knife deep into his bicep until the blade is bottomed out into his flesh. It takes a few seconds, but a deafening yelp breaks the silence.

Sadistic satisfaction acts like a drug, my body is buzzing from the justice I'm about to grant. He can hurt me and I'd sit and take it, but hurt my wife? You're six feet under and never seeing daylight again.

"Nice of you to join us!" I exclaim, faking delight.

I walk around so I'm facing him, trailing the knife along his collarbone as I move. Crouching in front of him, I pin him with intense eye contact. I feel his discomfort as he tries to look around the room, wiggling in his seat like an impatient child, but given the minimal light, he can only focus on one thing. Me.

"What's your name?" Pointing the knife an inch from his nose, I await his answer, but there isn't one. Moving the knife down below his collarbone, I press deep enough to draw thick blood. Crimson falls like a dripping tap, staining his white shirt.

Wailing mixed with pleads to stop breaks the growing silence, but it only encourages me more. I drag the knife until I'm at the tip of his shoulder, the lengthy slice oozing with no intention to stop.

"Name." I demand, placing my knife at his throat.

"Jerry!" His voice breaks, but he tries to suck in a breath to compose himself.

"Jerry," I repeat, nodding in confirmation.

A sinister smile grows on my face as I rise to my feet and turn towards the instrument table. Placing the blood soaked gutting knife down, my finger hovers from right to left, stopping on the bread knife. A simple household item, but painful if used in the wrong way.

Rhett stands with his arms and legs crossed as he leans against a hay bale, observing each thing I do. He won't get involved unless he needs to, he prefers being a watchdog.

"Hold that, will you? I need more access points." I pass the knife over to him as he reluctantly takes it from my grasp.

My feet carry me back over to Jerry. I bend and rip his thin cotton shirt, the fabric splitting as I tug. His bare chest is on display with no protective layer covering him, goosebumps attacking each inch of his pale skin.

My left hand darts sideways and Rhett places the knife in my palm. Swapping hands so the knife is in my dominant one, I plaster my rage inspired smile back on my face.

"Now, Jerry, would you please explain to me why I found you on top of my wife?" Images attack my mind of him flattening Claudia, touching her and using her against her will. I feel fucking nauseous looking at this sad excuse of a human being.

"Sh-she was askin' for it! I swear!"

Slice.

The jagged knife carves an unclean gash into his waist.

"Wrong answer." I growl. "Try again."

"She said she wasn't happy with you!"

Slice.

Although, that one could've been the truth.

But it doesn't warrant him touching her.

Another gash on the other side of his waist.

It's perverse that I'm enjoying this. I shouldn't be filled with pleasure when Jerry cries to God for help, or when his blood leaks from his vile wounds.

Claudia makes me feel a little murderous. I would never hurt her, but anyone who touches her isn't safe from me. I'll chase them to the end of the earth if they so much as hurt a thin hair on her head.

"Wrong again, Jerry! You aren't good at this game, are you?" I can't stop the laugh escaping my lips. But it's not funny. It's fucking outrageous.

"The truth, Jerry!" This time I bark, my face close enough to his that I can smell his fear.

Tears gush from his eyes as his mouth is wide open, gasping for breath.

Next technique on the list.

I turn and place the bread knife down and scan over my options. I want the truth, but I also want him to endure the torture he put my wife through. Not only did he violate her physically by touching her, but he's traumatized her emotionally and mentally. She didn't trust men before, and she definitely won't now. She'll endure a long healing journey; she doesn't deserve that pain.

He does, though.

I spot the medical gag and grab it, as well as pliers and the bowie knife. I give Rhett a nod to let him know I need his constant attention for this, to which he stands behind Jerry.

Shoving the medical gag into Jerry's mouth, he tries to fight it away with his tongue, but his efforts are pointless. With his teeth on display, I hold the pliers up, wiggling them so he knows my intentions.

"Untie one hand." I instruct Rhett.

Friction sounds behind Jerry before one hand is loose, and the other tied to the chair. I pass Jerry the handle end of the knife, and nod to him to take it. He does cautiously, unsure on why I'm giving him a weapon.

Like he sees a sudden chance, he jolts forward, waving the knife at me like a panicking child. Rhett's large hand grips Jerry's armed one and pulls him back, restraining him.

"That was cute," I mock, laughing at him. "Not gonna work though." I nod to Rhett behind Jerry. His look of defeat should be enough, but it's not.

"Here's what's going to happen. You're going to take that knife and stab your own thigh. If you refuse, I'm going to pluck your teeth out one by one, starting with the gold one."

Wide eyes filled with tears and a shivering body is enough to tell me how terrified Jerry is. He mumbles something, but I can't make out what because his mouth is pried open, ready for extraction.

"These are the consequences of your lies, Jerry." I shrug, feigning boredom.

Jerry pauses in false hope that I'm bluffing. Today's your unlucky day, Jerry. I don't bluff when it comes to my wife.

"If you'd rather me slowly and painfully extract your teeth," I trail off, clipping the pliers a few times as I lean forward.

Jerry's body shakes as he refuses, his eyes wide enough to pop out of his head. Slowly, he lifts the knife, his eyes closed as he heaves aggressively. With a sudden movement, the blade disappears into his thigh as thick blood pools below him.

"Again." I demand.

Stab.

"Again."

Stab.

"Again!"

Stab!

Deafening wails bounce off the metal walls like a call to all preying animals. All color drains from Jerry's face as his body weakens by the second. He breaks out in a heavy sweat as droplets gather in his receding hairline.

"Truth," I pull the medical gag from his mouth and yank the knife from his grasp, Rhett tying Jerry's hand back behind him.

Snot and tears mix together as they fall into his mouth. "I was tryin' to get to you." His admission is joined with sobs and quick intakes of air.

"Why?" I question, my brows pulling together in confusion.

"I wanted to hurt you the way you hurt me!"

I recoil, my eyes squinting at his admission. I've never seen this man in my life. How can I hurt someone I've never fucking seen before?

He must see my confusion because he gulps a deep breath of air before continuing. "The man on the bridge. Adam Cosby. That's my brother and you didn't save him!"

Piercing white noise blocks my hearing as my surroundings go foggy. My vision is black as I'm taken back to the worst day of my life. My worst nightmare circles on repeat in my mind, each second of that day a vivid memory invading my brain.

I choke on my breath, suddenly feeling trapped inside my body. Inside that dangerous loop I lost myself too.

Rhett's voice snaps me back to reality as I try to focus on the current and not the past. "You'd know that's not how it happened if you were there, Jerry. You weren't there for your brother, Julian was." Rhett tries to ease my sudden dread by telling me what so many therapists have already said. The truth is, it never gets easier.

"He could've saved him!" Jerry's tone has changed from pain to violence. "That's why I drugged her! I was goin' to fuck her, make her feel the pain I feel, make you suffer the consequences. I wanted her to scream for me to stop, just so I could fuck her harder. I wanted her to hurt as much as you hurt me, and when she asked why I did it, I would tell her it's all because of her pathetic husband!"

Each nerve ending in my body is numb. There's no single feeling inside of me except brutality. I want to hurt him; cause pain in areas he didn't know existed for even thinking of Claudia.

"Let me get this straight," Rhett growls. "You were going to rape an innocent woman, because you hate the man who tried to *save* your brother?"

"He deserves a lifetime of torment." Jerry looks dead behind the eyes as he stares through me, like he's already accepted his fate.

Violence turns my vision red. Each vulgar word from Jerry's lips plays on repeat in my head as I acknowledge everything he was going to do to Claudia. Bile burns my throat as a burning rage fires my body, using myself as a weapon.

"Don't you *ever* talk about my wife again." Perfectly composed, but my anger is the calm before the storm. I'm a volcano ready to erupt, and Jerry's words were all I needed to explode.

My fists connect with Jerry's cheek bones one after the other, each hit drawing more blood from his already pale face. Pain isn't present to tell me to stop so I keep going. I punch and punch, each hit met with a visual of Jerry fucking Claudia as she begs him to stop.

He *touched* her.

He touched what's mine.

He's going to die for that.

Crunches from Jerry's cheekbones fill the silent room as grunts of pain leave Jerry's lips. He's no longer conscious, but I have no intention of stopping. My fists are powered by their own minds as his face is stained with his own blood. My hearing is muffled and my vision is speckles of red from the scene I'm causing.

He's unrecognizable; his face swollen and bruised, leaking with blood. He gargles as he swallows his own blood, unable to beg for mercy.

It's psychopathic; I'm enjoying beating him. I'm getting a sick kick out of hurting him the way he hurt my sunshine. Hell isn't hot enough to punish a person like Jerry. I'll take his punishment into my own hands.

Rhett's arms are suddenly wrapped around my body, pulling me away and forcing me onto the hay bales. I grunt and shove, trying to break free of his grasp but my body is exhausted.

"Stop! Stop! He's nearly dead!" Rhett bellows, grabbing both sides of my face and grounding me.

My eyes flick to Jerry flopped lifeless on the chair. His chest is barely rising and falling, and his face is a bloated mess.

It's only now that I allow myself to breathe. To calm down and accept the person who hurt Claudia won't be able to hurt her again.

"Nearly murdering for her, now?" Rhett places a sheet over Jerry's body as he fiddles with the ropes, untying them.

Deep breathing so my heart rate slows down, I accept my actions. I did what I had to do for Claudia. For my family. For my future.

"He deserved what he got after touching my wife."

Rhett's statement is true, though. I've been in petty club fights, but nothing this bad.

"Go get your girl." Rhett instructs. "I'll clean this up. You want him dead or alive?"

"Dead." I deadpan, before walking away. I don't want to spend another minute away from her, so I take the opportunity and race home.

Desperate to feel the warmth from my sunshine in my arms, as all my problems evaporate in her presence.

18

CLAUDIA

Searing pain assaults my head as my eyes slowly adjust to the room brightness. I feel like I've been dragged through the forest by my hair and fought for my life after. Each part of my body aches as I struggle to move.

This is way worse than a hangover.

This is me waking up in Julian's room, without Julian.

I sit up, instantly holding my head as it throbs from the sudden movement. My eyes close as I wait for the pain to subside, but they instantly open again when I hear footsteps.

Julian approaches me wearing gray sweatpants, carrying a tray of tea, pancakes and aspirin. Popping it down in front of me, he slides back into bed and grabs the aspirin and a bottle of water from his bedside table.

"Drink." He demands, but his furrowed brows betray his usual blunt approach.

"Just because we're married, it doesn't mean you can tell me what to do." I try to stern my voice, but my throat is so dry, it feels like sandpaper. Reaching for the water bottle, Julian pulls it away from my grasp.

His eyebrows raise as he attempts to give me a stern look, but I don't miss the devilish smile he's trying to contain. "Nice to see you're back to your usual stubborn self."

"Stubborn?" I feign insulted as my hand is placed on my chest and my mouth falls open. "I think you're confusing me with yourself."

Julian's nose scrunches as he smiles and nods, but no witty comeback.

Phone the emergency services, there's clearly something wrong with him.

The dreamy smile that was there a second ago has suddenly changed to a worried expression, as Julian rubs the back of his neck. "So, we didn't get a chance to speak about last night."

Like I've suddenly been dunked under cold water, flash-backs of last night invade my mind like a chunk of information

I have to decipher. It's foggy and there are loose ends which leaves me with more dread than relief. Sometimes it's better to not remember the drunk antics you got up to the night before. But that's the thing, I wasn't drunk.

I remember the creepy guy at The Coven talking to me and guiding me outside, and I remember waking up in Julian's arms with Mr Creepy on the floor, but everything else is thick patches of blackness in my mind.

Oh no. *Did he?*

I suddenly feel dirty, knowing his hands have been on me. I feel ashamed not knowing what happened when I was taken outside. I feel embarrassed knowing Julian had to come save me, like a damsel in distress. If he didn't hate me before, he definitely does now. I'm a liability.

"Did he-" I trail off, unable to say what I'm wanting to. "When you found me, did he, you know-"

"No." Julian's firm response is met with his head profusely shaking. "I found you before he could do anything physical to you. But that doesn't mean what you're currently feeling is invalid, Claud. He took advantage of you and that's not okay."

Tears gather at my lash line once again and I don't even try to hold them back. It's like a dam has been opened and my built up emotions have been given the green light to run free.

Like a dripping tap, my tears fall one after the other, carving themselves a path to run down on my cheeks.

"Come here, Sunshine." Warm hands wrap around me, pulling me close to Julian's hard chest. "I'm sorry. I'm so fucking sorry for putting you in that situation in the first place." I feel his sharp intake of breath and his throat bobbing like he's holding back tears.

That makes me feel even worse.

I shake my head, not accepting what he's saying. "Don't say that, Julian-"

"I am. I shouldn't have let you leave."

I pull myself from his grasp and turn to face him. My head is still throbbing from the sudden change of position, but it hurts me to know he's hurting. It's like these rings on our fingers connect us further than a piece of paper. I hurt when he hurts. I smile when he smiles. I feel something deep in my heart that I'm scared to face, just in case he doesn't feel it, too.

"Don't." I grasp his hands and shake my head. "Please don't."

"Don't what?"

"Don't blame yourself when it's not your fault, Julian. I pushed the wedding forward and I didn't tell you about it. I'm the reason we argued yesterday. This isn't on you." I can barely get my words out without choking up. Thinking back to my actions, I want to punch past me for treating him this way.

"This is on me, Claud. Don't you fucking dare blame anyone other than me." His grip on my hands is strong as he pulls me closer. "My words were the reason you left. If I hadn't said it, you wouldn't have gone to The Coven and that prick wouldn't have drugged you."

The throbbing inside my head is getting unbearable, but I have to keep shaking my head to correct Julian's incorrect statements. "Not true. I would've gone to The Coven anyway. I couldn't stay here with the guilt of betraying you weighing me down. I could barely look at you when I came home."

"You're too good to me, you know that?" Warm, calloused hands heat my cheeks as Julian's hold on me is comforting. "I'm a shitty person and the only way I could be penalized is by punishing you. That's the only thing that could hurt me, so this is my karma."

"It wasn't your fault." I assert, grasping his bearded cheeks the way he grasps mine.

"Sunshine-"

"Shh," I place my finger over his lips. "Agree to disagree?"

His eye roll is enough for me to know I win this time.

"So, what happened to him?" I ask, taking the aspirin and water Julian hands me.

Julian clears his throat, and I instantly know it's not an answer I'm looking forward to knowing. My eyes widen and I silently pray for Julian to step in at any second and put my worries to rest, but he doesn't.

"Please tell me he's alive." My question is filled with false hope. I chuck the aspirin back my throat and gulp the cool water, hoping to wash away the unnerving feeling at the base of my stomach.

Slowly but firmly, Julian shakes his head. Zero emotion on his face.

Wide eyes and an open mouth is all I can muster. My mind is playing its favorite game of being jumbled and unable to make sense of anything.

Julian *killed* someone. He killed someone for me. Why am I not insanely scared of him right now? The hands resting on my thighs took a life. Were probably covered in warm, flowing blood that now belongs to someone who's dead.

I'm awaiting the fear or terror inside of me to blossom and force my legs to run, but instead, I feel weirdly reassured. Protected. *Safe*.

"I had no choice, Sunshine. He'll just keep coming back and I can't take that risk. I won't ever rest knowing your life's in danger." Julian's shoulders deflate as he looks down at his hands on my thighs, looking devastatingly guilty.

Squinting, I try to figure out what he's saying, but I'm no puzzle solver. "Why would he come back?" My stomach feels heavy as a moment of realization hits me. This isn't some small issue Julian has had to face. Whatever this is, it pains him.

A deep inhale enters his lungs as he readjusts both me and himself so we are laying on the bed. He places my head onto his chest as he draws reassuring circles on my back. "Six months ago, I was having a really shitty day so I decided to go for a walk around Casamount. I headed around the neighborhood, through the city, and found myself at the suspension bridge. It wasn't a busy day on the bridge, just me and a couple other people on their evening walks. I started making my way along the bridge when I noticed a man acting jittery. I just thought he was on drugs so I carried on." Julian releases a slow, shaky breath as he pauses for a second of composure. I can hear the pain in his voice by the increase in pitch.

"Each step I took, my gut feeling got stronger. It was telling me to go back and check on him, but I was stubborn and carried on walking. When I reached the end of the bridge, I finally gave in and turned around. Every step I took, I never even predicted what I was about to see. I wish I could've prepared myself, but no amount of preparation could have readied me for," he pauses, sucking in a breath before continuing. "That."

Constant circles on my back calm me, but nothing can ease the panic inside my chest. I already know where the story is going. Each part of my body aches for him, I want to take his pain and have it as my own so he doesn't have to carry the anguish anymore.

"He wasn't in the same spot, he was further down. He had climbed over the railings and was balancing on a thin piece of metal, completely out of my reach. I begged him to come back over the railings so we could talk, but he refused." Sniffling between words, I feel Julian's throat bob. "I asked why he was doing this, and his reply hurt so fucking bad. It hurt because it's fucking relatable. He said he was lonely. He was so alone, he had no one to share life with and no one to lean on. It hurt him everyday seeing couples, friendships, families, have a simple relationship that he craved."

We sit in silence for a few beats as Julian composes himself. "His name was Adam and in those five minutes I knew him, he was the sweetest person. I asked if he had family, and he said yes, and I thought 'great, that's a positive to fight for', but then

Adam told me he had a brother, but his brother cut all contact when Adam told him he was gay."

Julian's intake of breath is ragged as his voice breaks. I can't see his face, but I can feel his tears dampening my hair. It breaks my fucking heart.

"I told him I'm Julian and I'd love to be his friend. He said he would like that, but he doesn't want to burden me with his life. I tried to protest, but before I could get a word out, Adam jumped. He was dragged from the lake an hour later and declared dead at the scene." Julian pauses, the only noise around us is our sniffles and gasps for breath. "I was his last shot at life and I couldn't save him."

I lift my head, facing him. His red eyes are drowning in agony as they meet mine. He silently begs for reassurance, and I have a suspicion as to why we laid down. "Why couldn't I look at you while you told that story?" I whisper, my hand caressing his cheek.

"I couldn't bare the look of disappointment on your face."

Pain. paralyzing pain fills me as I finally see the absolute heartache Julian has to face everyday. "That's why you were drinking all the time? The paparazzi were basically just documenting your grieving journey."

Julian nods, his eyes unable to meet mine. "It gave the Grays a bad name. I promised my mother I'd make it up to her and the only way her and my uncle saw that happening was by getting married."

I nod, understanding, but I don't press for further answers as Julian's lost in thought.

After a long pause, Julian manages to look me in the eyes. "I still can't walk along that bridge." He shakes his head. Sitting up slightly, he holds himself back from touching me, but I don't let him. I need him to feel me, to know I'm here for him. "It elicited a new fear in me of being alone. I was scared I would be the same as Adam, so I drank the pain away. When we signed the marriage contracts, I was petrified you'd see me as the asshole that I had turned into. I had you followed because I thought I wasn't good enough for you and you'd find someone better."

Large hands pull me onto Julian's lap as he cradles me. His fingers intertwined with mine and delicate kisses are placed onto my head. "I'm still not good enough for you, Claud. But I'll spend a lifetime proving you're the best human to walk this earth."

My cheeks lift, my smile growing the longer Julian speaks. "Let me show you that life is worth living."

"I'd let you show me anything, as long as I have you by my side, Sunshine."

My nose scrunches at my given nickname. I've never understood where it came from. "Why sunshine? I haven't exactly been the best wife." I question, noticing Julian's eyes turn shy as soon as I ask.

"You're my sun. The one thing in my life that's always bright and shining, no matter the circumstances. I'm your moon, unable to shine without you. Together, we're an eclipse, celestial and powerful."

Swoon.

Warmth spreads throughout my stomach and I find my eyes brimming with tears again. Not sad ones this time, though. Pure elation, instead.

This is the side of Julian that his trauma has been hiding. It's the side he hides from the world, but he showed me. He ripped himself bare and put himself on display for judgment. But there's not an ounce of judgment inside of me.

I'm in awe of him.

Maybe that L word isn't so far-fetched after all.

19

JULIAN

I've woken up seeing clearly for the first time in over six months. This is the first time for as long as I can remember that I want to do something good for someone else. My own needs aren't my priority. Claudia's needs are, and I want to do everything in my power to make her happy.

It's a bizarre feeling, actually. I'm not used to feeling this vulnerable or exposed. It feels like Claudia is seeing past the hard exterior I've grown used to, and she can see a damaged, sensitive man instead. I'm not sure if I like it, but I'm fond of her, and because of that, my true self comes out in her presence.

She makes me want to be a better person. Being an asshole is part of my personality, but if there's one person I'll show my soft side to, it's her. That's why it felt so easy to explain my damaged past to her last night. There isn't a single person I've opened up to, other than giving Rhett the basics of what happened, but with Claudia, the words fell out of my mouth so easily. She has these adorable puppy dog eyes that make me want to give her everything she wants in life.

She deserves it.

I woke up with a face full of black hair and my sunshine's plump ass placed perfectly on my erection. If we didn't have a flight to catch, I'd be taking her right here, right now. But husband duties call, and there's nothing I want to see more than her surprised face when she realizes where we are going.

Untucking myself from my sleeping beauty, I chuck on some pants and make my way downstairs to my office. Flicking through my emails to see if anything important jumps out, I phone my PA, Ferne, and let her know I'll be out of office for a few days. She answers back, stating I'm never out of office when I always have my work on the go, but I make it clear I'm going to be off the radar and I have somewhere important to be. I don't miss her prolonged silence, and I know why she's speechless. I have never had a day off work. Nothing has ever been important enough to pull me away. Even when I was spiraling.

But there's a first time for everything.

I pack my case and check on Claudia, who's still sleeping. Her fatigue is more than likely from whatever drug Jerry gave her, so I let her rest.

"Magda," I call as hear her walking down the hallway. "Pack Claudia a case. We're leaving in thirty minutes."

She gives a nod of approval and is about to walk towards Claudia's room, but pauses.

I frown, unsure on why she's suddenly frozen like a statue, but I hear movement behind me, and I know what Magda is looking at.

"Are manners not in your vocabulary, Mr Gray?" Claudia's croaky morning voice is music to my ears as she pads from our bed to the doorway. Her hair is disheveled, her eyes not fully open and her lips plump. She's still wearing my shirt that falls to her thighs, and I take a mental picture of this moment. She doesn't need nice clothes and fancy makeup. She's perfection, twenty-four-seven.

I pull her into my side, her body cuddling into me, fitting like a glove. "Good morning, Mrs Gray. How are you feeling?" Placing a kiss on her forehead, I brush stray hairs from her face.

"Curious as to why we are packing. Offended from your lack of manners. Relieved it's because you're an asshole and not a bad person." Her nose scrunches after her statement as she tries to hide that adorable smile.

"Ahh, good. The Claudia I know is back in action." Her mouth opens to make a snarky remark, but I place my finger over it, shushing her. "Come on, we're going to be late."

Claudia's forefinger points at me as her eyebrows raise, feigning sternness. "I'm packing my own things."

Groaning out loud and tilting my head back, I try to hold in my laughter. Grasping her cheeks, I place a kiss on her lips before letting her go. The situation suddenly looms on me as I realize what I did. The way I feel about Claudia is crystal fucking clear, but expressing that to her? That's fucking terrifying.

She didn't pull away, though. That has to mean something...I hope.

We arrive at Casamount airport with two minutes to spare, which is an achievement considering Claudia was still dressed in my shirt less than fifteen minutes ago. I haven't seen her face since we got in the car because she's spent the whole car journey pushing her face up to the car window.

No matter how much she begs, our destination is a secret. It's almost fucking impossible to keep this a secret from her, but it'll be worth it.

It better be fucking worth it, because it's taking every ounce of power inside of me to not give in to her. Her bottom lip sticking out and her adorable eyes are tempting me to bend her over my knee and spank her.

"Your flight is ready, Mr Gray."

The traffic controller directs us to my private plane as the jets roar as they start up. I direct Claudia up first, but she refuses as she stands crossed armed, frowning.

"What?" I question, holding my hands out.

"This is not necessary, Julian! Why can't we fly like normal people?" I can see the mental debate she's having with herself. She doesn't want to change her ways and take advantage of my money, but her temptation is winning her over.

"Because I'm not normal." I deadpan, nodding to the plane stairs, but she still stays rooted, leaning her head forward for an explanation. "I'm Julian Gray," I step forward, grasping her hand, pulling her towards me. "And you're Claudia Gray, my wife. You deserve princess treatment. And it's a long flight, it would be even longer if we flew commercial."

She slowly moves forward, still putting on a front that she's not okay with this. "Fine, but if I have to fly private, you have to try economy at least once, for me. Promise?" She holds her pinky finger up, staring at me expectantly.

My eyes gaze to her finger, and then to her. "Seriously?"

"Seriously!" She wiggles her finger at me. "Don't be an asshole! Just promise me, please?"

How could I ever say no.

My pinky intertwines with hers. She kisses our fingers and holds them to me, waiting for me to kiss them. I do as her eyes tell me to.

"We have to lock it in." She says, shyly looking down at her feet.

"How do we do that?"

"We have to kiss." Stubborn Claudia is gone with the wind. She's replaced with nervous Claudia.

Grasping the back of her neck, I pull her close to me as my free hand wraps around her waist. She gasps at the sudden movement, but her wide eyes are paired with a cheeky smile. Closing the gap between us, I crash my lips to hers as we move in sync. Opening her mouth slightly, I slide my tongue in, welcoming her moans into my mouth.

I feel her legs weaken beneath us so I hold her up. I have to stop this before I rip her clothes off and fuck her on the runway. I'm so fucking desperate for her, I'd give everything up just to have my way with her.

Ripping my lips from hers, I ignore the hard erection in my pants and focus on Claudia. I take in her blushed cheeks and lust filled eyes, desperate for more. "We'll finish this later." I whisper in her ear, her lips letting out a needy gasp.

Suddenly, she's compliant, making her way up the stairs and taking a seat on the plane like a well behaved wife. If this is how she behaves when she's needy, then I'll be edging her more often. A disciplined Claudia is as good as a stubborn Claudia.

The seven hour flight felt longer than I hoped. Claudia spent the whole time asleep on my master bed, and I spent seven hours staring at her while she slept.

Creepy? Fuck yeah.

Do I care? Absolutely fucking not.

I'm too focused on keeping Claudia's eyes from knowing where we are. I pull a few favors and let them know the situation, and the airport was surprisingly understanding. I didn't even have to bribe them with money.

We get through passport control without any clues being given away and are in a blacked out private car before Claudia can go snooping. This car cost me a fuck load just to have the windows blacked out from the inside, just so Claudia couldn't peek outside of them.

"Can I have a clue?" Pleading eyes are pinning me with a glare as I avoid looking at Claudia.

"No." I respond bluntly as I flick through my phone.

"Julian, come on." She begs like her life depends on it. I'll remember that for later.

I shake my head, still not looking at her.

A warm hand is suddenly placed on my thigh and slowly makes its way upwards. My body is a lit match as heat courses through me. Claudia places her hand on my dick, but before she can make any further movement, I place my hand on top of hers. "Keep misbehaving and I'll fuck you until you can't walk." I growl, my nose touching hers.

"And that's supposed to be a threat?" Claudia answers slowly, unable to contain her smug smile. She can feel how fucking hard I am, and it's all because of her.

"We're here." Our driver announces as the car comes to an abrupt stop.

Claudia's teasing manor has suddenly changed to excitement as she looks out the black window. She releases a high pitch squeal as she tugs on my arm, but I don't move.

"Julian, come on! I can't wait!"

Slouching back in my seat, I spread my legs as I get comfortable, smirking at her.

Confusion racks her face, but acknowledgement suddenly hits her as her frowning brows are changed to a straight face and then, a glare. "No."

"Say it." I demand.

"No."

"Say it."

"No, absolutely not!" She flings her arms up, her stubbornness getting the best of her yet again.

"Fine, we'll go home and you'll never know the surprise-" I don't get a chance to finish my sentence.

"Please, Julian. Please show me the surprise!" She's practically bouncing around the car like she's on drugs. Her drug of choice is her excitement.

"Good girl," I praise, before getting out of the car.

I walk around to Claudia's side of the car and open the door. Before she can rise to her height, I wrap a tie around her eyes so she can't see. Her grunts of disapproval are cute, but aren't enough to make me change my mind.

Leading her from the car to the entrance, loud chatters echo around us. I note her heightened hearing is picking up every noise as she chaotically turns her head to each sound. Loud cars and horns fill the air as trees blow in the wind.

Pushing the doors open, we enter the museum, the sudden loud outside disappearing as we stand inside the foyer. The view is breathtaking, and I finally understand why Claudia has been wanting to come here. It's exceptional, unlike anything I've ever seen before. Stone walls and pillars with a central stone staircase leading off in two directions. Dated artifacts going back centuries before our existence. A large whale skeleton hangs from the ceiling with lots of archways leading off to different historical sections to explore. Golden lights brighten the room as the large ceiling windows offer natural light.

"Are you ready?" I ask, undoing the knotted tie.

"Yes!" She's erratic, desperate to see what I've been hiding.

Unlooping the knot, I pull the blindfold off and let her readjust her sight.

Wide eyes and an open mouth is all Claudia is able to do as she gasps. Her hand covers her mouth as her eyes dart around the room. Small droplets gather on her lash line, and I panic.

Is she crying?

And are they happy tears or sad ones?

Shit, what have I done?

"Oh my god, Julian. You brought me to the Natural History Museum?" Her words are barely audible as more tears fall from her eyes. Her body is almost frozen as she stands in shock, and I decide in this exact moment that this was a really fucking bad idea.

Claudia shakes her head as she looks at me, and I accept my fate. I've fucked up so bad, she's never going to forgive me. But, instead, she jumps on me, grasping me. "Thank you, thank you, thank you! I don't even know what to say, other than we need to explore, because I have so much I want to see!" Her hand grasps mine, pulling me down the staircase. "Come on!"

Six hours later, our tour around the Natural History Museum is completed. Who knew Claudia had enough energy to pace around this old building without needing to sit down once? Not me.

I'm fucking knackered, but there isn't a single part of me that wanted to stop this tour. Watching her eyes gleam at every display piece was all the energy I needed.

Standing back at our starting place, Claudia rests her arms on the railings, looking over the staircase. I stand next to her, observing. My eyes roam over her expressions, each one delicate and precious. There's a whole world of emotions going on behind her eyes, and I'm lucky enough to witness them first hand.

"I want to get married here." Claudia's eyes are lost in thought as she glances over the museum.

"We could've, but you chose the courthouse." I tease, earning myself a shocked expression. Claudia's hand is in motion to shove me, but I catch it before contact is made. Her shocked expression suddenly changes to instant regret as her eyes widen. She sucks in a breath, realizing her plan didn't work out, and now there's repercussions.

"Tsk, tsk, tsk." I shake my head, yanking her closer to me. Our bodies are flushed, our heat acting as one source. "Act recklessly, suffer the consequences, Sunshine."

In one swift movement, I grasp her thighs and sling her over my shoulder. Her chuckles echo throughout the almost silent museum as she wriggles in my grasp. She earns herself a sharp spank on her ass, squealing from the punishment.

"You're lucky I booked a hotel across the street. This couldn't wait any longer." I groan as I stride across the street to our hotel. My cock throbs with each step I take, my patience running impossibly thin.

Thank fuck Ferne already checked us in and got our room code. There's no fucking way I'm wasting time talking to people when I should be balls deep inside my wife instead.

We enter the elevator and I press our floor button as we start ascending. Claudia wriggles and tries to free herself from my grasp, but I don't let go. Instead, I slide her down my front, so her legs are either side of my waist and her pussy is in line with my erect cock. Our chests are in sync as they rise and fall with each pant, unspoken words hanging between us. I can't hold on, I need to taste her.

"Fuck it," I groan, grasping the back of Claudia's neck and pushing her against the elevator mirror. Crashing my lips to hers, my blood runs hot as it reminds me how painfully hard one human being can make me. Only Claudia could make my dick misbehave like this.

Claudia moans as she opens her mouth, allowing my tongue access as I lick and taste. Kissing a path down her neck, I rip the front of her dress open, exposing her bare tits. My mouth latches onto her taut nipple, a gasp escaping her perfect mouth. I suck and flick as my fingers find her free nipple, pinching it between my fingers. They're hard and sensitive, so I nibble one before sucking it better.

Fuck me, this is the longest elevator ride I've ever been on.

Remembering the tie I have in my pocket, I pull it out and hold it in front of Claudia. She nods, and I tie it over her eyes.

Placing Claudia on the floor, I trail my hand down her stomach, tucking my fingers below her tights and panties. Flicking her clit, her body reacts to my instantly, arching her back and gripping my shoulders. I move my hand lower, feeling how fucking soaked she is for me.

"Be a good girl and let me fuck you with my fingers." I tease her entrance, gathering her juices before bringing my fingers to my mouth, tasting her. My eyes close as I savor the taste. "My wife tastes so fucking good." I groan.

"Yes, Julian. Yes." Whimpers leave Claudia's lips as she begs for my touch.

In one swift movement, I slip my hands below her waistband and plunge two fingers into her. Moaning, Claudia cries in pleasure, saying words in Spanish that I don't understand.

I finger fuck her at a constant pace, her body reacting like she was fucking made for me.

Smashing my lips to hers, I drink in her moans and gasps as I pick up the pace. I feel her legs begin to shake as she grasps onto me for stability, but I don't stop. Her pants become more erratic as her pussy clenches around my fingers. "That's right, baby. Come for me."

Her hand smacks over her mouth as she tries to muffle her own moans, but I grasp her wrist and hold it above her head. "I want to hear how good I make you feel." I tell her, fucking her through her orgasm. Her legs quiver as her moans turn into a lyrical song. My hand dampens as Claudia comes all over my hand, her pussy throbbing around my fingers.

Panting in sync, I remove the tie as Claudia comes down from her high. I remove my hand from her pussy, earning myself a whimper at the loss. An explanation is on the tip of my tongue, but the never-fucking-ending elevator finally comes to a stop and the doors open, revealing some corporate looking men.

Their eyes dart to Claudia, who is fully clothed but her dress is ripped down the middle, so she holds both bits of fabric together awkwardly. Her cheeks are already flushed a pretty shade of pink, but the embarrassment nearly turns her into a tomato.

I don't like how they're ogling her, so I give Claudia my jacket and cover her exposed areas. I guide her out the elevator, giving those pricks a stare sharp enough to cut. But they don't get the hint.

"Stare at my wife again and I'll feed your eyeballs to you." I play my favorite staring game, which seems to shoo them off with gasps and shocked expressions.

Now they're out of my way, I sling Claudia over my shoulder and stride to our room. I punch in the code and kick the door open, but my patience is no longer present. And neither is Claudia's, evidently.

Sliding her down my chest so she's back with her legs on my hips, I press her back against the wall, ripping off the jacket I just gave her, along with the rest of her clothes. Claudia does the same to me, lifting my shirt over my head and unbuckling my belt and button.

Spinning her around, I place Claudia on the bed beneath me, her body naked and fucking perfect. Her tits are a perfect handful and her nipples are pink and erect. Delicate curves down her waist and hips, and her thighs are my favorite thing to grip onto.

"Fuck," I groan. My cock can't take this. It's so fucking hard already, but staring at a flawless Claudia whose bare and waiting for me? I'm about to come right now.

She clearly thinks I'm taking too long admiring her, because she sits up and yanks my pants down, my dick springing free. Her mouth opens as her eyes widen like she hasn't seen it before.

"What?" I question, confused by her reaction.

"Nothing," she shrugs. "Just mentally comparing you to my blue friend."

I waste no time grabbing her and sitting on the end of the bed, bending Claudia over my knees. "Count." I demand.

I lift one hand up and spank her right ass cheek. She gasps, but I can see the wetness gathering at her entrance.

"One."

Spank.

"Two."

Spank.

"Three."

Spank. "That one was for marrying me in a fucking court-house." I grunt, spinning her around and placing her below me on the bed.

"That was deserved," she admits through blushed cheeks, her eyes pleading, but I'm not sure what for. "Sex, please."

My eyes drink in her delicate features, my stomach swarming with butterflies. I stroke stray hairs from her face, and I readjust myself so I'm lined up with her entrance. "You sure?" I ask.

She nods.

"Words, Sunshine."

"Yes," she responds breathlessly. "Yes, I need you."

That's all the confirmation I need. Feeling her wetness gather on my tip, I thrust into Claudia in one pump. We gasp in unison, both of our eyes focused on where our bodies meet. I give her a second to adjust as she closes her eyes, but Claudia gives me a little nod after a few seconds to proceed. Thrusting in and out, lewd noises fill the air of our sex; erotic and passionate. "Taking me so well, baby." I praise, my eyes meeting hers. My lips hover over her lips, our pants in sync with each thrust.

I bring my thumb pad to her clit, circling it in a constant motion. Her back arches at the movement, allowing me to suck a nipple into my mouth. I flick and bite, earning myself loud moans and whimpers from Claudia.

I can't hold it in anymore.

"Fuck, Claud. You know I love you, right?" The words slip from my mouth before my mind agrees to it.

"Julian, oh god." Her hands are placed on my back as she claws her way down. "If you mean that, you'll tell me afterwards."

The way she says my name has me nearly coming, but I use all my fucking willpower to control myself. I pick up my pace, thinking about nothing other than telling this woman how I really feel. Loud slaps echo throughout the room from our bodies clashing together. Claudia's pussy tightens around my cock as her eyes flutter shut. "I'm going to come." She whispers, before pleasurable screams fill the room.

"Fuck, me too, baby. You're too fucking perfect." My vision starts blurring as heat builds inside my core.

Perfectly in sync, we reach our highs at the same time. We're on that blissful cloud of pleasure, each nerve ending in our bodies flicking with electricity as we pull towards each other. This type of sex is a drug; addictive and obsessive. The kind of feeling that has your eyes feeling too heavy to open and your body too weak to move. The euphoric feeling that has you needing another fix as soon as you finish, because the whole experience feels too good to be true. I feel numb, but in the best fucking way.

"Is it true?" Claudia's delicate voice pulls me from my after-sex daze. I slump next to her, pulling the duvet over her naked body and sliding in next to her.

"I wouldn't lie to you, Claud." I brush my fingers down her cheek as her big, blue eyes gaze up at me. "The way you make me feel is unlike something I've ever felt before. I didn't think I was capable of feeling this way about someone; the whole love thing has always been a foggy subject for me. I never understood how people could push their own needs aside for one person, but the way I feel about you, Claudia, is crystal fucking clear. I'm so in love with you, I'll spend the rest of my life trying to be the husband you deserve." The words fall from my lips easier than I expected. It took no rehearsals, no scripts, just words true from my heart.

Claudia's eyes fill with tears, and I realize she's teared up way too many times today. I'm stuck in apprehension, waiting for her response. "Sunshine," I press. "Are you okay?"

"No." She shakes her head, but a grin grows on her precious face. "I've been in a loop of uncertainty the past few days, torturing myself into believing we wouldn't get a happy ending."

Confusion racks my body as I try to make sense of what she's saying. "Uncertain of what?"

"That you'd never feel the same way about me that I feel for you. I thought there's no way you'd ever forgive me for what I did to you, let alone love me the way I love you." Heat blooms in my core at Claudia's confession. "Julian, my heart beats for you. I don't want to face life without you by my side." Tears fall from her eyes, so I wipe them away with the pad of my thumb.

I feel like I'm in paradise, being given the life I don't deserve but so desperately want. I can't control my face from beaming at Claudia's confession. I'm fucking elated, nothing could ever top this.

"Fuck, baby." I grasp her cheeks, placing a deep kiss on her plump lips. "I fucking love you."

Her sweet giggle fills the room as she places her hands over mine, kissing me back. "I fucking love you too, asshole."

So, dreams do come true. They're just usually disguised in a marriage contract and a bossy woman.

Sounds like heaven to me.

Epilogue

CLAUDIA

Six months later

"**M**amá, I'm nervous." The statement falls from my lips as I examine my reflection in the archway mirror. Off the shoulder, long sleeves glittered with hundreds of Swarovski crystals, a slim fit full length dress with a short train. My wedding dress is exactly how I planned it. Subtle makeup and loose curls, with my dark locks tucked behind my ears, pair perfectly with my ivory vale.

"Hush, Claud. You're already married." My mother's abrupt tone is warranted as she checks over my outfit.

"Are you still mad I didn't tell you about him?" I plead, taking my bouquet from her and holding it up in front of me.

My mother releases a deep sigh, her warm hands grasping my cheeks. "Baby, I know what it feels like to be in love. Me and your father met when I was traveling in South America and met in Argentina. I thought it was never going to work between us; I'm American and I guessed he'd want to stay in Argentina, but love took control and pulled us together." She releases my face and grasps my hands. "What I'm mad about is you didn't tell me about him until six months ago, when I could already tell you were both head over heels for each other."

I shake her off, trying to hide my smile. I get why she's mad, I used to tell her everything, but since Julian, I've been a little secretive. My parents don't know when me and Julian met, when we actually got engaged or married, and when I moved in with him. They met him after our trip to London and assumed our relationship started from me working 'away from home'. I told them we got married on a whim, but we had history so we weren't strangers. If they knew the real story, I'd have to explain the rent situation and it would all unfold like a web of lies. They're clueless and happy, and I'm going to keep it that way.

"I'm sorry, Mamá. Some things just happen!" I shrug, my tone abrupt from the jangling nerves inside of me. I spot the glass of champagne that Amalie just poured and snatch it up in a second. Gulping, I invite the bubbly liquid into my stomach, wincing at my burning throat.

Three light knocks rasp on the door, Amalie screaming at them to not come in until she checks, because she doesn't want Julian appearing. She cracks the door open, peaks, and then opens it wide to my father standing there, looking dashing in a suit.

"Are you ready?" He questions, his expression soft.

I nod, my brows pulling together as my cheeks lift.

Hold those tears back, Claud.

My father holds his arm out for me to link, so I grasp onto him like any little girl does with her daddy. My mother and Amalie scramble downstairs to get their seats while me and my father take a moment to breathe.

"This place is beautiful. I'm so happy your dream is finally coming true, Nena. You deserve it." My father's eyes examine our surroundings, every inch of the walls in this building worth studying.

When Julian told me we were marrying at the Natural History Museum, I laughed at him. It took him an hour to convince me it was true, and when I finally believed him, I fainted. Once I regained consciousness, I started bawling. Julian thought it was because I hated the idea, but truthfully, it was the complete opposite. He's given me everything I want, need and dream of, like I'm living in my own fairy tale. He doesn't realize the only thing I need to make me happy is him.

Violin chords echo down the halls, playing a sweet, upbeat wedding entrance song as all of our guests wait in the main hall. I saw the setting plans before our guests arrived, and I almost choked on air. For our ceremony, there are rows and rows of white chair seating with gorgeous floral statues placed around the room. Wisteria hangs from the above whale and the central white aisle has light blue petals scattered for my descent.

For the wedding breakfast and evening celebrations, floral decorated circular tables replace the seating rows and the natural daylight is replaced with beaming stage lights. Faux blossom trees are placed around the outside of the dance floor, giving a colorful, naturistic feel to the room.

Two of my favorite things in one room; history and Julian.

My father gives my hand a squeeze as the violins get louder and we make our descent down the staircase. It takes me a couple seconds to take in the amount of attendees that are here, but my eyes only look out for one person.

My husband.

Julian

It feels like the air has been smacked out of my lungs when my eyes fall on my bride. A herd of emotions takes over my body, my heart takes control and lets my feelings have free reign. Tears warm my eyes as they gather in my lash line, falling down my cheeks.

I can't pull my eyes away from her. She's mesmerizing. Ethereal. Exquisite. Mine.

We may be standing in a large building full of loved ones, but my brain doesn't acknowledge them. It feels like it's just me and Claudia at this moment. Our moment.

That's the beautiful thing about this wedding; love pushed us to do this. Our hearts are so in sync that we feel the same for each other. We're destined to be together, like the gods made us a perfect fit for one another.

If you told me nine months ago that me and Claudia would be having an actual wedding because we're so sickeningly in love, I'd have laughed. But I'd have probably been nicer to her, knowing what the future held for us.

I can see now that Claudia is a blessing in my life. I was desperate and lonely, and when someone was finally in my corner, I pushed them away as a defense mechanism. Claudia has a big heart and will do anything for the people she cares for, including pushing those who stand in her way. Luckily for me, I'm now one of those people she cares about.

Claudia's father, Felipe, passes Claudia over to me, giving me a handshake and a nod of acceptance. He's like the father I never had. He's taken me in as his son-in-law and has treated me with nothing but respect. I may have a small hole in my heart where a father's love should be, but Claudia and her family give me enough love that my father isn't even a passing thought in my mind.

My eyes trail down Claudia's body, taking in every tiny detail. "My beautiful wife." I whisper in her ear as I grasp both her hands opposite me.

"Julian," she murmurs, her bottom lip popped out and her brows pulling together. "Don't make me cry."

The officiant starts reading his script as our guests take their seats and focus on us. We read each other so well, mine and Claudia's eyes meet, both our cheeks lifting. Her eyes are blue like the ocean and leave me feeling breathless. It's hypnotizing; I get lost in a world of Claudia, and it's my favorite place to be. It's sunshine, flowers, history and laughter, and that's my own personal fucking heaven.

Claudia may say this marriage benefitted her, more so than me. She got more out of it, securing her family's future. But the truth is, I'm the one who benefits from this marriage the most. I get a friend, confidant and wife all in one. I have someone to make those tough days easier. I have someone who brightens up my day when I'm miserable. I have someone who will open her legs so I can feast on my favorite thing in the whole world, my wife's pussy.

Vows are spoken and cheers erupt as soon as the officiant clears his throat. "You may kiss the bride." I waste no time. Grasping Claudia by her neck and waist, I dip her and smash our lips together, sealing our bond once and for all.

Power play is what the press have been calling it. Claudia has access to my bank account, my home, my car. They're all hers. But all that shit means nothing when she owns my fucking heart. My whole world is Claudia Harper Gray, and I'll spend every single day proving to her what a miracle she is.

I'm no prince charming, but she's a princess, and she'll be treated like one for the rest of her life. Because she's my wife, and my wife gets whatever the fuck she wants. And if she can't get it? I'll burn the world to the ground until she does.

THE END

Acknowledgements

Where do I start?

Fiancé, as always, my number one supporter and favourite human on this entire planet. None of this would be possible without you constantly encouraging me and making me believe in myself. Those back tickles are for sure my favourite thing to keep my brain firing away. I love the little face you pull when I explain story lines and characters, it's like you're trying so hard to understand but it's just going over your beautiful bald head. You're my true blue and I love you endlessly.

P, my right hand man when it comes to needing some encouragement. I'm grateful to always have support from you and for writing in caps when I tell you a plot idea. I imagine you screaming your excitement at me and it gives me a massive boost every time. I can always count on you to be there for me no matter what, and because of that, I'm eternally grateful you're my person.

My pup, for those constant kisses and cuddles that keep me going. My baby girl, always.

My siblings, who always do little squeals and always smile when I tell them I'm writing. I love you guys.

Ria, you're an absolute star in this often dull world. Hearing words of encouragement coming from you mean more to me than you could ever know. I'm so grateful to have you on my book journeys with me. I 100% couldn't do it without you. Thank you for everything!

Jules, for creating such a gorgeous book cover! And for letting me buy book covers before I even have the story written (oops).

All my author friends who have always been there to give me support and advise. You're all amazing! (Especially you, Cecillia, ilysm!)

My BETA's, Bree, Lærke and Elizabeth. Your advice is so valuable to me and I couldn't have done this book without you. Bree, your word docs, as always, are the most amazing thing an author could receive. Claudia wouldn't be who she is without your in depth feedback, and for that, I'll forever be in debt to you! Lærke, your voice notes made me smile and laugh so much! You helped editing my first manuscript so much easier! Elizabeth, your keen eye to spot those mistakes was a lifesaver!

ARC readers, as an author, I cannot thank you enough for wanting to read Power Play! Thank you so much for showing interest and applying. Your messages and insta posts fill me with so much happiness and warmth. You are truly the best.

And finally, my readers. Readers are the reason us authors have a place in the crazy book world, so thank you so so so much for reading my words on paper. You guys will never understand how important you are to me. I hope you enjoyed Power Play, and once again, thank you so much for reading my second book baby.

About the Author

Esme Lennon is an indie author from England. Her love for reading first started on Wattpad, where she read a few too many Marvel fanfics, and also began her writing journey. This led Esme onto booktok, immersing her in a world of contemporary romance and dark romance books. This gave her the courage and inspiration to write her own books and explore her own fictional worlds.

In her free time, Esme loves to lose herself in a good book and spend time with her fiancé, friends, family, and her pup. She's a complete home bird; you'll find Esme snuggled up on the sofa, re-watching Marvel movies with her better half.

Also By

Fancy reading about a stalker and his little snowflake? Read Little Snowflake now! Available on KU and in paperback.